Hanover House

Hanover House
© 2015 Brenda Novak, Inc.
Cover Design by Croco Design

Also by Brenda Novak

THE SECRET SISTER

A WINTER WEDDING*

THIS HEART OF
MINE*

THE HEART OF
CHRISTMAS*

COME HOME TO ME*

TAKE ME HOME FOR
CHRISTMAS*

HOME TO WHISKEY
CREEK*

WHEN SUMMER
COMES*

WHEN SNOW FALLS*

WHEN LIGHTNING
STRIKES*

IN CLOSE

IN SECONDS

INSIDE

KILLER HEAT

BODY HEAT

WHITE HEAT

THE PERFECT
MURDER

THE PERFECT LIAR

THE PERFECT
COUPLE

WATCH ME

STOP ME

TRUST ME

DEAD RIGHT

DEAD GIVEAWAY

DEAD SILENCE

EVERY WAKING
MOMENT

COLD FEET

TAKING THE HEAT

*Whiskey Creek Stories

Look for Brenda Novak's next novel
Discovering You
available June from MIRA Books!

Hanover House

"The psychopaths are always around. In calm times we study them, but in times of upheaval, they rule over us."

—Ernst Kretschmer

by
New York Times Bestselling Author

Brenda Novak

Prequel to HER DARKEST NIGHTMARE,
to be released
from St. Martin's Press in 2016

To Dan Raines, my agent, for all of his big ideas.

Dear Reader,

I'm so excited for you to try the kick-off to my brand new suspense series with St. Martin's Press. Like Evelyn, the main character in this book, I've always been fascinated by psychopaths. I want to know why they exist, why they do what they do and if they can ever be treated and reformed. These are questions that have stymied psychiatrists and psychologists for years, but Evelyn is determined to do all she can to solve the riddle of the psychopathic mind. I guess creating her was one way I could study the subject and learn along with her (as funny as that may sound). I have to admit, the research has been fascinating.

HER DARKEST NIGHTMARE, the next book in this series will be released September 2016, and the book after that will be out in February 2017. So you are starting at the very beginning. I hope you find it to be a grand adventure.

I love to hear from my readers. Please feel free to contact me with any comments or questions at www.brendanovak.com. There, you can sign up for my mailing list so that I can alert you when other Evelyn Talbot Chronicles are released, check on the many titles in my backlist (I've now written over 50 books!) or enter my monthly prize drawings. Or maybe you'd like to contribute to my efforts to raise money for diabetes research. So far, through my annual online auctions and various other fundraising efforts, I've managed to raise $2.5 million (my youngest son is Type 1; I would like nothing more than to find a cure for him and all the other people out there who are grappling with this terrible disease).

Here's hoping you enjoy your visit to small town Alaska —and Hanover House, home to some of the worst serial killers on earth!

Brenda

"The psychopaths are always around. In calm times we study them, but in times of upheaval, they rule over us."

—Ernst Kretschmer

Prologue

California...

HE'D FOUND WHAT he needed. At last. After twenty
years of waiting, of planning, of purposely blending in
to escape notice, he had the thread that would lead him
back to the only woman who'd ever really mattered in
his life.

The only woman who'd ever been a challenge.

The only woman who'd ever gotten away.

Once his parents had finally gone to bed, and long
after anyone would expect for them to have a visitor,
Jasper Moore stared down at the envelope he'd
recovered from his father's desk. Inside was a letter
from Evelyn Talbot's father, pleading with Stanley and
Maureen to come forward if they possessed *any*
information on Jasper's whereabouts. It said that Evelyn
had been through enough. That the Moores should
finally do the right thing and divulge any information
they possessed. But they never would. They were the
ones who'd helped him escape in the first place, all
those years ago—and they told everyone they hadn't
seen him since before the murders, even though, in
recent years, he'd risked a furtive visit now and then, if

he could do it safely.

Anyway, it wasn't the letter that concerned Jasper. He didn't give a shit about the Talbots' emotional plea for justice and closure.

He was far more interested in the return address on the *envelope*.

Chapter 1

Four months later...

SHE'D BEEN ATTACKED. Dr. Evelyn Talbot remembered that right off. From the lights and the noise, she also knew she was in a hospital. She just couldn't recall how she'd gotten there.

"She's moving. I think she's coming around."

Was that a doctor, or maybe a nurse? She didn't recognize the voice, but her thoughts were fuzzy, and it was too difficult to open her eyes. She almost sank back into the dark void she'd just emerged from, where she could drift without worry, without having to conjure up the chain of events that had led to this. She didn't want to fight any of the battles she'd have to fight if she woke up.

But then she heard a voice she *did* recognize, and that voice spoke directly to her.

"Honey, it's Mom. Can you hear me? If you can hear me, squeeze my hand."

Squeeze her hand? Surely, things weren't *that* bad. But Evelyn didn't yet know for sure. She could hear tears in Lara's voice, so she felt obligated to expend the Herculean effort required to actually break the surface of consciousness.

"She's pretty drugged. It might be a while," the first person responded, but that person didn't realize how much Evelyn stood to lose if her family started to make too much fuss about the risk inherent in her job. What'd happened today (if it was still "today"; she had no idea how long she'd been out) was her own fault. She knew the type of men she dealt with, understood what they were capable of. She'd studied more psychopaths than almost any other mental health professional in America. She'd merely allowed herself to be distracted at the worst possible moment.

"Mom?" she croaked, forcing the word through lips that would barely part.

"Evelyn!" Her mother leaned over her bed. "You gave us such a scare. Are you okay?"

Lara's white hair and gently lined face, pinched with worry, finally came into focus. A nurse was in the room too—a young Indian woman with a kind smile—but no one else. Where was her father? And her sister? Surely, Lara had alerted them.

Wait...she wasn't thinking straight. Of course they wouldn't be here; they'd be back in Boston. Her mother had traveled with her to San Francisco, where she'd had to come on business, so that they could spend some time together before Evelyn moved to Alaska.

"I'm fine. Everything's...fine." At least, she hoped it was. It would help if her darn tongue wasn't so unwieldy... That was due to the pain meds, no doubt;

she recognized the effects. "What happened?"

She remembered leaving her mother at the hotel, arriving at San Quentin State Prison, passing through security and waiting to meet with one of the candidates on her list—a serial killer who'd strangled fifteen women...

Hugo Evanski. That was his name. She'd been standing up, reading his file when he was brought into the room, and then...nothing. That was where her mind went blank.

"That animal you went to see?" her mother said. "That murderer? He broke away from the guard and rushed you on sight. Hit you so hard you banged your head against the wall, then fell and hit the corner of the desk. You have several stitches in your temple."

Evelyn licked her lips, trying to ease the dryness. She felt like the tin man from *The Wizard of Oz*, with no oil. "Did he...did he do anything else?"

Lara's eyebrows knitted. "Isn't that *enough*?"

"I can't feel much. I'm...trying to ascertain the extent of my injuries."

The nurse lifted Evelyn's arm to take her blood pressure. "According to your chart, you have a concussion and six stitches," she said and gave her hand a reassuring rub before putting air in the cuff.

"They got him before he could do any more damage," her mother explained. "But you hit your head so hard that they had to check your brain to see if you were hemorrhaging."

Not good news. "Am I?"

"No. Thank God."

Evelyn drew a deep breath. "Then I'm going to be okay, like I said."

"*This* time," her mother responded. "But what about next time? What if something like this happens in Alaska, and they can't pull the bastard off you soon enough? Or if you're hurt even worse and they can't get you to a hospital because of severe weather? Why you'd isolate yourself up there, in the wilderness, with so many human monsters, I have no idea."

Evelyn couldn't miss this opportunity, even if her mother didn't like the idea of her living so far away. It was the culmination of her professional aspirations. "I didn't get to choose where they built the facility, Mother."

The nurse removed the blood pressure cuff, made a notation on her chart and said she had another patient she needed to check on.

"They tried other locations," Evelyn went on as the nurse hurried out. "Texas. Arizona. South Dakota. Hilltop didn't protest quite as much." With only five hundred people in town, they couldn't have the political influence of a larger community, so even if they'd gone at it with more determination, it might not have made the same difference. But she didn't add that. Neither did she volunteer that public opinion hadn't shifted in the facility's favor until after Hilltop had been adopted as the building site. It seemed as if those in the "lower forty-eight" liked the idea of stashing their worst criminals all in the same place, as long as it was some *other* place.

"Heaven help the people who live there," Lara muttered.

"They won't need heaven's help." She stifled a groan for how difficult it was just to talk. "Hanover House is going to be a level 4 facility. All the...the monsters will be locked up."

The lines in her mother's face grew deeper. "And you'll be inside with them."

They'd been through this... "My office will be in a whole other wing."

"You'll have to go to the prison section to observe or meet with your subjects."

"When they're brought to a session with me, they'll be wearing cuffs, ankle bracelets and a belly—"

"Like this guy was? The man who just hurt you?" her mother broke in before she could qualify that statement, as she'd planned.

"Yes, but...I wasn't expecting him to act as he did. He'd barely walked into the room. I had no idea he'd rush me so quickly."

Her mother's hands, with the cuticles around her nails torn up from the way she constantly picked at them, tightened on the bed rail. "Where was the guard, for crying out loud?"

Evelyn allowed her eyes to close. "The officer who escorted him didn't expect it, either, I'm sure—or he...would've been more prepared."

"So what are you saying? *Whoops*? It won't happen again?" The pitch of Lara's voice shot up an octave. "What if this psychopath had had a homemade weapon? A shank or whatever they call it? He could've stabbed you. *Killed* you. Is that what you're *hoping* will happen? What Jasper did when you were in high school was...beyond a nightmare. After surviving such a horrific ordeal, why wouldn't you do everything possible to avoid men like him? I mean...what are you thinking? Do you have some kind of death wish?"

Evelyn opened her eyes and managed a scowl. Surely by now her mother should know that what she did wasn't really a choice. She *had* to do it; couldn't do anything else, not after what'd happened when she was only sixteen. She'd found her best girlfriends brutally murdered—all three of them! She'd almost been killed by the same boy. After three days of torture, Jasper Moore had slit her throat and left her for dead—and it wasn't as if he'd been a mere stranger. He was her high school boyfriend, someone she'd trusted enough to give her virginity.

But she was still struggling against the debilitating effects of the meds they'd given her, so all she could say was, "No. Of course not."

Lara's head jutted forward. "Then why must you surround yourself with conscienceless men who'll do anything to hurt other people? Lust killers? You've told me yourself that they take pleasure in causing pain.

You're only thirty-six years old, Evelyn. And you're so beautiful! Regular men trip over their feet when they see you. Of course the sickos behind bars are going to fixate on you."

Many of her opponents had pointed to her gender, age and physical appearance as reason she shouldn't be working in the criminal justice system, especially in such an impactful way, but she wasn't about to tolerate that bias. "Those are all things I can't change. I...I am what I am, but I won't let the fact that I was once...terrorized get the best of me." She could feel the pain in her head growing stronger but she was slowly regaining her faculties and was too caught up in what she wanted to say to pay that dull ache any attention. "At some point, we simply *have* to...to come to understand *why* psychopaths act as they do. How they come to be. How to stop them." She drew a bolstering breath. "Only then can we protect the innocent."

"And what if there are no answers?" That her mother spoke through her teeth gave evidence of her deep-seated anger—and the fact that Evelyn hadn't gone through her painful ordeal alone. "Sometimes there isn't a reason for what people do!"

"There's *always* a reason, Mom." Evelyn had to swallow to be able to continue. "Besides, the more we try to ignore the psychopaths who live and work around us, hoping they'll...they'll go away on their own, the more...the more power people like Jasper will possess." She allowed the volume of her voice to drop. "And the more people they'll hurt."

Lara's dangly earrings swung as she shook her head. "But there's no understanding crazy!"

The degree of her belief in what she was about to say gave Evelyn an added shot of adrenaline. "I've told you before, Jasper wasn't crazy and neither are the men I study. If there's one thing I've learned, it's that."

Her mother straightened. "I don't care if they're sane or not. I don't even care if there's a great need for your work. You've done enough. You've convinced the government to build this study facility. Now let someone else take over. *Don't go to Alaska.*"

Still struggling to maintain the clarity she needed to continue this argument, Evelyn shifted in the bed. "I have to."

"*Why?*"

"Hanover House will need me in order to succeed. Nobody else seems to feel quite as passionately as I do—and, let's be honest, I've been the driving force behind it from the beginning."

"Why not let one of the other members of the mental health team you've assembled take over? Dr. Fitzpatrick has fifteen years on you, much more experience, and he's a man—not someone those ghouls will be likely to salivate over and dream about raping. Let *him* take the lead."

She put a hand to her forehead, felt the bandage. "He'll be a great help. I couldn't have brought Hanover House into existence without him. But I won't relin-

quish control of what I've worked so hard to create."
Not when she was so determined to find the answers
she craved: Why was there such a thing as a psychopath? How did such people come to be? Was it nature,
nurture or a combination of both that created this
fearful anomaly? Was the rate of psychopathy increas-
ing, as some studies indicated? And how was it that
such people could very often kill their own mothers, or
even their own children, and not feel a second's
remorse?

Evelyn's curiosity about those things in particular
drove her worse than a relentless thirst. And now that
the government had agreed to build a high-security
federal institution where she and a team of other
psychiatrists and forensic psychologists could make an
in-depth study of those for whom murder was a delight
instead of merely a means to an end, maybe she'd
finally find out what made them tick.

Her mother sank into a chair. "What's it going to
take to get through to you? Jasper's still out there,
Evelyn. He could see you on TV or hear about your
work in the papers and take it as a personal challenge to
find you and finish what he started twenty years ago. Do
you realize that?"

She'd *had* to lobby publicly, shame lawmakers into
doing more to protect victims like her. She couldn't let
her fear of Jasper and what he might do stop her. That
would only render her useless. She felt like she'd lived
through that ordeal for a reason, had to make it mean

something. "I can't let that stop me."

"Yes, you can!"

"No." At this point, her head was *throbbing*, but Evelyn had to make her point. "He murdered my best friends simply for telling me he cheated on me! I found them, Mother! I *saw* what he did to them! I refuse to care more about my continued safety than I do about what he did to all of us—and what others like him are getting away with every day."

Lara seemed dazed now that most of the fire was gone from her anger. "But working in this field makes and keeps it all so present."

"I've had plenty of therapy to help me deal with it." She didn't add that there were *still* some nights when she woke up in a cold sweat, convinced that she was lying on the dirt floor of that old shack, her body bruised and broken, the blood pumping from the wide gash in her throat, creating a warm puddle around her. But she knew her mother wasn't fooled.

Although Lara sat without speaking, she turned a pointed gaze on Evelyn, burying her beneath an avalanche of disapproval.

"Why are you letting our trip to San Francisco go this way?" Evelyn asked, breaking the silence. "Are we going to end up fighting about this, like we always do?"

Her mother pursed her lips but seemed to soften a little. "At least tell me that you're not going to have the inmate who did this shipped to Alaska."

Evelyn recalled the brief glimpse she'd had of the

man who'd shuffled into the room before he rushed her. No doubt he thought such a demonstration of his "evil" would scare her away, make her set her sights on someone else and leave him in sunny California.

But that was precisely the reason she wouldn't go to Alaska without him.

"No. He's going with me."

The blood drained from her mother's face. "You can't be serious..."

"I won't let him get the best of me," she said. "Not now. Not ever."

"You mean like Jasper did."

She ignored that. "Hugo Evanski's ideal for my program."

"You're letting it get personal, Evelyn."

"*He* made it personal. And as soon as I get out of this darn hospital, I'm going to tell him."

Chapter 2

TO HIDE THE fear that slithered, snake-like, just below her skin, making the hair on her arms stand up, Evelyn paced across one end of the small, concrete cell, pretending to be absorbed in her notes. It'd taken a few days, but she was back at San Quentin, and they were bringing Hugo Evanski to meet with her. Only this time she was prepared for anything he might do—and so were they. The warden had told her that Evanski would be escorted by two correctional officers instead of one, and he wouldn't be allowed to get out of control again.

When he didn't appear as soon as she'd expected, however, she set her notes aside and leaned on the desk to draw a deep breath. She'd only been released from the hospital two days ago, still had a bandage covering her stitches and a black eye to show for that earlier incident—embarrassing proof that she'd allowed herself to be hurt by someone she'd known was dangerous. There was no excuse for that, especially because her detractors wouldn't hesitate to use what Hugo had done to undermine her efforts, if word ever got out. She had to be careful about what showed up in the press; she couldn't allow Hugo Evanski to jeopardize a program that was still in its infancy and needed time and support in order to grow.

When a clang signaled she'd soon have company, she snatched up her notepad so that no one would be able to tell that her hands were shaking. Although she told herself that the same thing wouldn't happen twice, no amount of self-talk could overcome the emotional response that welled up whenever the slightest sound, smell or other trigger reminded her of what Jasper Moore had done twenty years ago. And Hugo's attack definitely reminded her of Jasper. Just about any violence did.

She watched as the heavy metal door slid open and two hulk-like correctional officers walked their charge into the room. They tried to seat him in the steel chair bolted to the floor, probably so that he couldn't launch himself at her again, and, when he stiffened instead of bending, forced him into it.

"Sit your ass down," one of the guards growled.

Hugo gave his chains a rebellious jerk but eventually complied, lifting his nose in the air and smiling at her as if he was too preoccupied with and delighted by what he'd done to her face to be bothered by correctional officers who were determined to show him they were in charge. "Looks like you've had an accident," he said to her.

She fingered the tender spot near her temple. "It's nothing. Someone of your reputation...I would've expected you to be able to do a lot more than simply knock me into a table."

When the two officers on either side of him barked out a laugh, obviously surprised by her response, the smile disappeared from Hugo's clean-shaven face. "Maybe it won't go quite so well for you the next time."

Evelyn's heart was racing so fast she could scarcely breathe. Like Jasper, this man wouldn't hesitate to kill her if he had the chance. But she leaned forward anyway. "There won't be a next time, Mr. Evanski. I'm not stupid enough to allow you another opportunity. At least, you'll have to work a lot harder for it than you did a few days ago. I merely wanted to come by and tell you to pack up whatever few items you possess."

"You're having me transferred to Alaska?"

"You're brighter than you look."

The clenching of his jaw gave her some satisfaction. He wasn't pleased by this news, as she'd guessed he wouldn't be. She'd just let him know that he wouldn't control her, certainly not through fear. If she had to guess, that bothered him, too. He wouldn't like a woman having any authority over him. But, oddly enough, even when he was angry he didn't look overtly dangerous, didn't look much different than the middle school teacher he'd once been—before his wife stumbled upon the body he'd temporarily stowed in the shed of their cabin in Bakersfield, California. As a matter of fact, he was *so* plain Evelyn would even call him nondescript. He had short, dark hair and, after ten years in prison, no scars or tattoos, no evidence of gang affiliations. He wasn't even particularly muscular, not like so many of the other inmates she saw as she visited various institutions—those who spent the majority of their time lifting weights.

Maybe that was why he'd blended in for so long, why no one had suspected him in the murders of the young women he'd killed even though he'd taught them all in school and had, at two different points, inserted himself into the various police investigations.

The only thing that might've tipped anyone off was his eyes. They were brown, not black, but they were just as cold and lifeless as a shark's. He seemed to have that in common with other psychopaths. Difficult as it was to define, there was always *something* about the eyes. They held no light, no *humanity*. Evelyn had heard many victims state the same thing and, as a victim herself, she could attest to the truth of it—at least she'd noticed the lack of emotion in Jasper's eyes once he'd turned on her and revealed himself to be the homicidal maniac he really was. Before that, she'd detected no appreciable difference between him and the other boys at school.

Anyway, Hugo didn't need to *look* mean. He'd proven his capacity for violence in a way she wouldn't soon forget. The warden had told her he was *so* cunning and cruel no one dared mess with him. He rarely responded at the time of a confrontation, but he always figured out a way to get even afterwards.

The warden had also said he spent the majority of his time reading, writing or creating clever cartoons parodying law enforcement, which was the reason Evelyn had put him on her list to begin with. He was smart. She couldn't help thinking he might be able to teach her something none of the other psychopaths she'd studied could—by being self-aware enough to analyze his own actions or describe his mental processes in less vague terms.

"You don't want me in Alaska," he said.

His voice held a low warning, but since the interview had progressed as she'd hoped so far, Evelyn was feeling a little more confident and a little less shaken. "Because you're so dangerous? Was that the message you were sending me?"

When the guards chuckled again, a muscle moved in Hugo's cheek. He had an overinflated view of who and what he was—most psychopaths did—so he didn't take kindly to being laughed at. "No, I hit you for the fun of it."

"But don't you see?" She put down her clipboard. "That's precisely what makes you such a great candidate for my program."

"Studying me would be a waste of your time," he said. "I'm no different than any other man."

"You scored a thirty-seven out of forty on the Hare Psychopathy test—"

"Which means nothing," he broke in. "That test is a joke."

The test wasn't perfect by any means. It'd been highly criticized, even by people in her own profession.

And, if it wasn't properly administered and applied, she could see the potential damage it could do, how much it could hurt someone to be improperly labeled a psychopath. But the PCL-R, as it was called, did give mental health professionals—and prison staff too—something to work with to make sure they were all talking about the same traits.

"I'm not here to debate the work of my predecessors," she said with a wave of her hand. "Suffice it to say that as far as I'm concerned, a thirty-seven makes you quite different, considering the average score for all incarcerated male offenders in North America hovers around twenty-three or twenty-four."

He wiggled his fingers as if to depict a ghost or other spook. "And once you pass the magical number of thirty, you're categorized a monster. If it were that easy to identify people like me, people like you would be out of a job."

"Now *you're* over-simplifying," she said mildly. "The test has proven successful in calculating recidivism and other things. So why don't you stop playing games? You murdered fifteen women without compunction, fifteen women who once attended the middle school where you taught. That can hardly be called average."

"They shouldn't have resisted my...ministrations," he said with a shrug. "I warned them that I was their master, and they would submit to everything and anything I wanted, or else."

"Making what you did *their* fault?"

"You could say that."

"No. Only *you* could say that, which is why you scored so high on the PCL-R. You don't take responsibility for your actions."

Leaning back, he crossed his ankles. When the chain linking his feet rattled, the two correctional officers tensed, in case he was about to get up, and yet the movement came off quite civilized, as if he was merely sitting in a restaurant, about to have a cup of coffee. "I've seen you on TV, you know."

That didn't surprise Evelyn. Most people, at least anyone who'd ever had any interest in the criminal justice system, had seen her on TV. Like her mother said, that probably included Jasper, if he was still in the States. But it was a risk she'd had to take. "I'd guessed as much. That explains your rather...aggressive behavior from the other day, doesn't it?"

He watched her from beneath half-lowered eyelids. "Alaska doesn't hold much appeal for me."

She could understand why. Living behind bars was difficult enough. Very few of those she'd selected for Hanover House *wanted* to be sent to Hilltop, a small town an hour outside of Anchorage, where it would be that much harder to maintain contact with friends and relatives on the outside. Besides the isolation, fear of the unknown (since her program was the first of its kind), and the lack of sunlight during the long winter, they would have less chance of escape, the hope of which kept some men going. Even if an inmate of Hanover

House somehow managed to slip outside the prison, and the perimeter fence surrounding it, there'd be nowhere to go.

"I may be a hunter," he said, "but Alaska has *less* women, not more."

She arched her eyebrows to put him on notice that his words didn't shock or discomfit her. She'd heard far worse. By the time the psychopaths she worked with came into her sphere of influence, intimidation was the only string they had left to play on, so they became masters at it. "On the other hand, there *are* plenty of places to hide a body."

A wry smile twisted his lips. "Now you're speaking my language." He clasped his hands in his lap. "Tell me something..."

She perched on the edge of her chair. "What's that?"

"Do you really think you can do it?"

"Do what?"

"Figure me out. Explain why I *like* to kill—why I'd do it again if I could."

"We'll never know the answer to that question unless I try. And you might be encouraged to hear that there will be certain benefits to moving to your new home. You won't be locked up in your cell ninety-nine percent of the time, for one."

"Because I'll be doing what?"

"There will be an abundance of studies and other activities for you to participate in, many of which will offer incentives that could make your time in prison easier than it would be here."

He didn't respond right away. He studied her for a few seconds. Then he said, "Will I get to spend much time with you?"

She felt the creeping sensation he, no doubt, hoped to inspire. She often became a focal point of her patients, especially *these* sorts of patients. But that type of thing came with the territory. "Most likely. Dr. Timothy Fitzpatrick, also a psychiatrist, is lending his support to the project. He and I will head up a team of seven psychologists. With only a little over two hundred subjects, there will be a reasonable ratio of mental health providers to inmates." She hoped both her team and the number of psychopaths in the study would grow with time, that the breadth and scope of her studies would one day become quite extensive, but she had to start somewhere—and this was her shot.

His gaze slid down, over her breasts and hips as if she stood before him naked. She wore a skirt, blouse and heels. She'd gotten blood on the only suit she'd brought to California when she hit her head last time, or she would've worn it again. Typically, she tried to avoid anything that showed her legs. She received enough sexual interest from the men she studied as it was. She didn't care to encourage that—although it was inevitable no matter what she wore. They didn't come into contact with many women, especially women under the age of forty.

"I have to admit, it's beginning to sound interesting," he said. "But may I ask what, exactly, you're studying, Dr. Talbot?"

Dr. Talbot? He'd switched tactics. She got the impression he was trying to charm her, trying to engage her beyond the usual scope of the interview. But she was equally curious about him, so she was willing to play along—to a point. "All aspects of behavior, but... speech patterns would be a specific example."

"Because...?"

"The patterns of those who score high on the Hare Psychopathy Checklist—men like yourself—tend to combine words differently than others. I find those differences fascinating and would like to see if I can establish more of a link, discover why."

He rolled his eyes as if that sounded positively boring. "Who cares about speech?"

"*I* do. It could lead us to other discoveries." Studies had already shown that psychopaths sometimes had difficulty monitoring their speech...

"You're willing to risk your life to figure out why I speak differently than you?"

"Someone's got to do it."

He made a clicking sound with his tongue. "Good Lord, you're foolhardy. Can you imagine what might happen with so many ruthless killers under one roof?"

She'd been confronted with these scare tactics before—not only from the psychopaths themselves but from her detractors in the media. "There will be plenty of security, I assure you."

"Doesn't matter." He shook his head as if she didn't quite get it. "All it takes is *one* breach, and...it'll be a bloodbath."

Evelyn folded her arms. "The potential alone should fill you with excitement. Have I convinced you? Are you now eager to join me in Alaska?"

The corners of his lips turned up. "Absolutely."

Chapter 3

JASPER MOORE HAD changed his identity several times over the years. He now went by the name Andy Smith, which was far more common and unremarkable than "Jasper." He'd changed his face, too. Considerably. So considerably that sometimes he regretted the surgery. But he'd probably be in prison right now if he hadn't taken advantage of what his parents had afforded him.

Although he was home alone, he made sure the door to the bathroom was locked before taking the tattered old prom picture from his wallet. He was a fool to keep anything that connected him to the past. But he hadn't been able to let go of this one item. Not only was he the boy he used to be in that photograph, which he sort of missed, Evelyn was with him. It was the only tangible thing he'd had to remember her by during all the years he'd waited to come into contact with her again.

Filled with longing, he touched her face. Studying it brought him such exquisite pleasure, so much that all of his victims looked like her. The woman he'd picked up last week especially. From a distance, he would've sworn it *was* Evelyn.

Too bad the bitch had opened her mouth and ruined the illusion...

"Andy? I'm home!"

Shit! He'd thought he had another hour, at least, before his wife got off work. After leaving the woman who was bound and gagged at his little hideaway, he'd spent too much time watching Evelyn's parents' house, hoping her mother or father would lead him to where she was living these days.

"Hey, where are you?" Hillary called.

With a grimace, he put his precious picture back inside the secret compartment in his wallet and turned on the shower so she'd think he was unavailable. He didn't care to see her, didn't want her to bring him down with her complaints about his inability to maintain steady employment. After he'd found that envelope from Evelyn's parents in his father's study, he'd convinced her to move to Boston by telling her he'd been promised a good job there. So she wasn't happy that in the month since they'd been living in Massachusetts no job had materialized.

She'd also be angry that he hadn't picked up her two brats from their friends' house after summer camp...

She surprised him by knocking instead of waiting until he was out of the bathroom. "Andy?"

When he didn't answer, she knocked louder.

"Andy!"

He quickly removed his clothes and stepped into the

shower so he could respond without sounding as if he was right on the other side of the door. "What is it?"

"How'd your interviews go?"

"Not so good," he replied.

There was a pause as she dealt with her disappointment. "What went wrong?" she asked at length.

"I'd rather not talk about it."

"So you didn't collect the girls?"

"My last interview ran late, and after hearing so many no's, I wasn't in the mood to see anyone."

There was another long silence. She used to show some sympathy, tell him he'd have better luck tomorrow, that she loved him anyway, that sort of thing. But she was becoming less and less understanding. Now she *wanted* to let him know that she wasn't happy with the kind of husband he'd turned out to be.

He wished she'd leave, just walk away and start dinner. He was hungry. Or she could go get the kids, if she was so damn worried about them. But she didn't. He heard her voice again. "Can I come in? I'd like to talk to you while we have some time alone."

And air all of her complaints? He'd had enough of that. "Not right now," he said. "Can't you give me a chance to rebound a little first? I feel like shit as it is."

Besides, he hadn't yet had the chance to wash up properly after leaving the woman he was keeping in the shack he'd built. It was going to take some time to get all the blood out from under his fingernails...

✦   ✦   ✦

IT WAS LATE when Evelyn's father picked them up from Logan International Airport. Grant embraced them. Then he took one look at her stitches and cast a sidelong glance at her mother, who'd no doubt spent every minute Evelyn had been preoccupied with work complaining to him about what'd happened at San Quentin and how it could so easily happen again in Alaska.

"How was the trip?" he asked as he put the luggage in the back of the SUV.

Lara didn't answer even though the question had been thrown out to both of them, so Evelyn jumped in. "Necessary. Informative."

Grant closed up the back. "But did you have any *fun*?"

Evelyn couldn't claim it'd been fun. Instead of the enjoyable shopping, eating and sightseeing experience she and Lara had hoped for, it'd been strained, especially after that incident with Hugo. Her mother would look at her and shake her head, or she'd reach out and touch the bandage covering Evelyn's stitches. Most of the time, she wouldn't say anything. A stark expression conveyed her concern. But if they *did* talk, the conversation invariably turned to Hanover House and her work and why she insisted on doing what she did.

"I'm glad we had some time together before I have

to leave," Evelyn said, trying to remain positive.

"Speaking of leaving, how much longer do you have left—five weeks?" her father asked.

"Only four."

"That's coming right up. Do you have to do more traveling before you go, or will you be home until you move?"

Evelyn got into the back seat; her parents climbed into the front. "I have to go to Pennsylvania next week, but at least that isn't as far away as California."

"You've been working so hard," he said. "You're determined, I'll give you that."

She *was* determined. She'd had to be, or that experience with Jasper would've destroyed her. The memory was always there, a constant threat to her peace of mind. Maybe that was why she fought so hard every day. Her parents didn't realize it, but she was hanging on by a very thin thread. If she didn't continue to march forward, and take more ground in her battle against psychopathy, she was afraid she'd backslide into the broken person she'd been right after the incident, despite all the counseling and hard-won self-healing.

Besides, what else was there for her except work? She couldn't meet a nice man, fall in love and start a family, like other women. Jasper had seen to that when he'd destroyed her trust of the opposite sex.

"It's taken a tremendous amount of effort to make HH a reality," she said, but even 'tremendous' seemed like an understatement. Not only had it been necessary to sell the need for such study to the right politicians, she'd had to petition for the funding, research the psychopaths who might be able to teach her the most, and recruit a mental health team she believed in *and* who were willing to follow her into the wilderness— literally and figuratively. And, while she did all of that, she'd had to prepare for the move by closing down her psychiatry practice, putting her condo up for sale and having a bungalow built on the outskirts of Hilltop so that she'd have a comfortable place to live when she arrived.

Fortunately, the bungalow was ready and waiting for her. She'd stayed in it and furnished it when she went back to hire the warden who would be running the prison side of the facility. She was just waiting to have the alarm system installed, and the contractor she'd hired had promised it would be in before she moved there.

"We'll help you pack, of course, but"—her father pulled through the gate surrounding her complex— "what are you going to do if the condo doesn't sell before you have to go?"

"I'll have no choice except to leave it empty and hope my Realtor will be able to sell it after I'm gone."

"I guess that type of thing isn't too uncommon." He parked in a visitor's stall. "Let us know if we can do anything to help."

Although she wasn't excited about covering two house payments, she earned enough to make it possible, so she refused to stress over the condo. Part of her was tempted to rent it out, anyway, in case she didn't like Alaska and wanted to come back. But she was afraid that having a bail-out plan might make it too easy to give up. "I will. Thank you. I appreciate the support."

"What's the latest word?" Grant asked, his hand on the door latch. "When will Hanover House be finished?"

She released her seat belt. "We're hoping to open November 1st."

"You're going back so early, I thought that must've changed."

"No. I need to help the warden staff the place, and that'll take a while. I plan to be fully prepared when my subjects arrive."

"You mean the murderers, rapists and con-artists who are currently incarcerated elsewhere," her mother supplied.

At the bitterness in Lara's voice, her father reached over to rest his hand on her mother's knee. It was meant to be a comforting gesture, but he didn't say anything and neither did Evelyn. Thank goodness the "fun" trip with her mother was over. Now she just needed to unwind and get some sleep before she had to start another day with an endless list of details.

"I'll get your luggage," Grant said and climbed out.

Evelyn stared up at the light shining through her living room window. She left it on whenever she was gone. Because she was so eager to get a break from her mother, it beckoned to her, promised solitude. But the thought of being alone also made her uneasy. As cautious as she tried to be about keeping her personal information private, she couldn't live completely off the grid and continue to be a fully-functioning individual. She wouldn't sacrifice a normal life for anything, not even safety. That meant there would always be some way for the men she worked with to find her.

Only a few years ago, an ex-con she'd once evaluated for the Massachusetts Department of Corrections had broken in and nearly raped her before her neighbor heard all the thumps, bumps and cries. The police arrived in time, but Carl Jenkins, her attacker, would never reveal how he'd come by her address. His silence on the subject sometimes made her wonder if she'd overlooked something obvious, something Jasper could easily dig up...

Stop. That was the paranoia talking. Jasper had to be living abroad. After all the money she'd spent on private investigators, and the many, many times she'd followed up with the Boston Police Department, demanding they do everything possible, they would've found him by now if he was in America.

Her father rapped on her window as he carried her suitcase to the sidewalk. "You coming?"

She was tempted to ask if she could spend the night with them. She was *so* tired. She wanted to feel safe for a change. But such an admittance would only convince them that she wasn't doing as well as she pretended. So she got out and opened her mother's door to say goodbye. "I hope you're not going to stay mad at me."

"Maybe I will," her mother responded with a pout. "Why do you have to worry me so much?"

"When I suffer, you suffer. I get that. I'm sorry I didn't turn out to be a...a nurse or a real estate agent. But...as long as Jasper's still out there, would *anything* be safe?"

Her mother said nothing.

"I believe in my work," Evelyn added. "Knowledge is power."

Lara held out for another second. Then she pulled Evelyn into her arms and hugged her fiercely. "*Please* be careful."

"I will." Evelyn breathed in the familiar floral scent of her mother's perfume. "I promise. You know I have a gun inside, and I know how to use it."

When her father brought her suitcases into the house, Evelyn almost asked him to look through every room, even the closets, despite the fact that her security system indicated no one had been inside the condo since she'd been gone. The little girl in her still craved Daddy's protection, she supposed. But she'd quit having him do stuff like that after graduating from college, when she'd bought her Glock.

"Your mom loves you, you know," he said.

She nodded, absently looking for anything that might be out of place. "We'll work through it."

He propped his hands on his hips as if he might say

more. But he must've realized that nothing would convince her to change her mind. She was going to Alaska no matter what. So, after a sigh, he put his arms around her.

"We *both* love you," he said. Then he was gone and she was left to lower the blinds and listen to the settling noises of her condo while wishing she'd insisted they take the time to stop by her sister's to pick up her cat. The house felt so empty without Sigmund...

Evelyn wondered how many women, like her, had to feel afraid, even inside their own homes. Probably not a lot per capita. But there were other survivors out there. They understood.

She took her gun from the kitchen drawer and went through her nightly ritual where she checked every nook and cranny that could possibly hide a human being. Only when she felt confident that no one was going to jump out at her did she put her gun on the counter, slip off her shoes and turn on the TV.

The nightly news came on. She watched for a few minutes, trying to relax so that she could sleep. She wanted to see if anything about her experience at San Quentin would be reported. But hearing about a missing woman and then a murder downtown didn't help her anxiety. She kept glancing at the darkness beyond her windows, wondering if someone was out there—and if that someone might try to get in before morning.

She'd just walked over to fix herself a drink when

her phone rang.

The Alaskan area code told her it had to do with Hanover House. It was four hours earlier there, so not too late to be calling someone. But Bob Ferris, the warden she'd hired, had taken his family to Hawaii for two weeks, before he had to start work in earnest, so who could this be? A member of the mental health team who'd gone to Alaska to oversee the building of his or her home?

"Hello?"

"Dr. Talbot?"

The deep voice on the other end of the line gave the caller's identity away before he could provide his name. It wasn't a member of the team. It was Benjamin Murphy—or Sergeant Amarok, as the locals called him— the handsome Alaskan State Trooper who served as Hilltop's only police presence, other than the two part-time Village Public Safety Officers he designated each summer to help him enforce the hunting and fishing regulations, which was the bulk of his job.

"Sergeant, what can I do for you?" She caught her breath, feeling that odd rush of excitement that came over her whenever he was around. She wasn't often attracted to someone like she was attracted to him—and had been from the first moment she'd set eyes on him. Especially someone who didn't particularly like her in return.

"I'm afraid there's been some vandalism at the prison," he replied. "I received a call from the construction crew this morning, and went out to have a look. I left you a voicemail, but when I didn't hear back, I thought I'd better try again."

She'd been flying all day, hadn't yet checked her messages. "*Some* vandalism?" she echoed nervously. She didn't need trouble. What she was trying to accomplish was difficult enough...

"Yes. The copper pipes, tubing and wiring have been ripped out," he explained.

"That sounds more like theft."

"Except they didn't steal it. They dumped it on site. And they smashed the windows on the office side, knocked over the portable johns, which created a sickening mess, and spray-painted the walls with...I'll just say...unfriendly messages."

"Geared toward who or what?"

"'Keep your crazies in the lower forty-eight,' that sort of thing, only with slightly more explicit language."

"So it was directed at *me*."

"Since one word began with a 'C' and was used repeatedly, I can only assume whoever did this wasn't directing their remarks to the men involved in this project."

"I see." She rubbed her arms, feeling chilled even though it wasn't cold. Some of the people in Hilltop were leery about the kind of facility she was building in their backyard, but it was primarily Sergeant Amarok who'd revealed express opposition. Did that mean anything here? It certainly jumped out at her right away. He'd lobbied against the prison—quite vocally—until the mayor and a handful of other key citizens managed to convince him to back off for the sake of the jobs Hanover House would create.

At that point, Amarok had gone silent, as if he'd considered himself outvoted, but Evelyn wasn't under the illusion that he'd changed his mind. He didn't want her in his town. He scowled if they ever happened to bump into each other, or had occasion to attend the same meeting—and there'd been several instances when she'd found it necessary to sit down with the mayor and the city council, as well as various prominent Hilltop "influencers."

Once, when she'd gone to eat at the local diner, Amarok had been there too. She'd thought he might approach her, as a professional courtesy if nothing else, but he hadn't. He'd remained in his own booth, watching her as if he didn't trust her a whole lot more than she trusted the psychopaths she studied.

"Do you have any idea who might've done it?" She wondered how much it was going to cost, and if this would mean they'd have to delay the opening. That certainly wouldn't help her new venture get off to a smooth start.

"'Fraid not."

She was trying to decide if he was taking any pleasure from this unfortunate occurrence, but that wasn't easy to determine over the phone. "Interesting..."

"Why would it be 'interesting' as opposed to some

other word?" he asked.

"Because the only person I can name who hasn't been excited about the benefits of having such a tremendous influx of federal money injected into the local economy is..." She caught herself before she could actually accuse him. She was reacting to the sting of rejection she felt as a result of that graffiti, and the fact that she didn't want someone she was attracted to knowing—or telling her—that she wasn't wanted. It wasn't often she experienced the kind of sexual awareness Amarok evoked. At least 6'2", with broad-shoulders, a muscular build, thick black hair and the most gorgeous blue eyes she'd ever seen, he was beyond handsome. All he had to do was look at her to make her weak in the knees. But she had no romantic notions where he was concerned. She hadn't had sex with a man, with anyone, since Jasper. He'd ruined her in that way, made it impossible for her to overcome the memory of his abuse long enough to become intimate.

Besides, if she had to guess, she'd say Amarok was only twenty-seven or twenty-eight. That meant he was nearly ten years her junior, which made even *dating* him unlikely.

"Because the only person you know who isn't excit-ed you're coming to town *is*..." he prompted.

She could tell he wasn't fooled, that he knew exactly what she'd been about to say. "Never mind. Are you-are you going to look into it? Will you try to find those responsible?"

"Of course." He sounded offended that she'd even ask. "Whether I'm excited to have Hanover House as my new neighbor or not, it's my job to protect it now that it's here. I'm calling you to suggest you get some security, though. It's a miracle whoever trashed the place didn't take that copper."

Suddenly far more fatigued than she'd been a moment earlier, she rubbed her face in spite of her makeup. "Since they left it, I'm guessing they were trying to make trouble, not money." And if the press printed something about it, maybe they would be successful. Sometimes it only took a spark to start a firestorm, which was why she'd been so worried that what Hugo had done would reach the media.

That could still happen, and now she had to worry about this too. But she'd known, when she first set out to establish Hanover House, that it wouldn't be an easy undertaking.

"I agree," he said. "Problem is they could always change their minds and decide to get a bit more out of it. Or someone else could come along, now that it's such easy pickings. I can't sit out there around the clock and guard it. I have other responsibilities."

When she said nothing, his voice softened. "Did you hear me?"

"Yes. Thank you for calling."

He didn't hang up right away. "Are you...okay?"

That he could tell she wasn't feeling her best surprised her. That he'd asked rather grudgingly didn't.

"Of course." She put more effort into speaking stridently, confidently. "I'll be fine. I've come this far, haven't I?"

"When will you be back here?"

She thought of her trip to Pennsylvania next week. If she flew to Alaska as soon as possible, maybe she could offset any future troubles before they cropped up and return in time to keep her appointment with the prison that caged the next psychopath on her list. "I'll be there as soon as I can catch a flight."

"You're not going to let *anything* stand in your way, are you," he said.

It was a statement, not a question.

She let her breath go in a long, silent sigh. "No, I'm not."

Chapter 4

SHE WAS DEAD.

"Andy Smith" frowned as he gazed into the sightless eyes of his latest victim. He'd been planning to kill her eventually. But he'd expected to have a few more days to play with her.

Damn! She'd spoiled his fun. How could he have thought this woman to be anything like Evelyn? This bitch didn't have *half* the strength. It'd taken less to kill her than any of his other victims—except the girl he'd kidnapped from the bus stop in Georgia. That one had had diabetes. He'd been curious to see what would happen to her without insulin, so he'd removed her pump—and found out within twenty-four hours. Once she'd gone into a coma, it didn't matter how much insulin he injected. He couldn't get her out of it.

He paced back and forth across the dirt floor of his hideaway. What should he do now? He'd been so excited to arrive this morning, so relieved when Hillary had agreed to put the kids into an "after camp" program so he could attend the "technical training" he claimed to have registered for. She didn't expect to see him until dinner, which gave him all day.

So maybe he'd have some fun with the corpse.

He sat next to it on the old iron bed. He supposed he could see if there was any satisfaction to be gained. As far as he was concerned, she deserved whatever he could devise. Normally after a kill, he experienced such a tremendous release that he could go months before the tension began to build again.

But she'd denied him that, left him hanging—and after he'd gone to the trouble of building this damn shack so that it would be almost identical to the one where he'd kept Evelyn. He wished he could've built in the same spot, but even if it wouldn't have been risking too much, there were houses there now. The most he could do was drive through the area every once in a while and allow himself to enjoy the memory.

He'd never experienced anything more fulfilling or gratifying than those three days with Evelyn. The look of shock on her face when she found her friends dead had been priceless. And that first rush of freedom, when he'd decided he'd do whatever he wanted regardless of what anyone had to say about it... Wow!

After cutting the woman's hands and feet loose, he took off the blood-encrusted gag. Then he removed the banana he'd shoved into her rectum. He had something else he planned to put there, wanted one final hurrah...

But his body wouldn't cooperate. This dead woman no longer appealed to him, no longer reminded him the least bit of Evelyn, so he didn't care to touch her. He figured he might as well vacuum her body with his battery-powered vacuum, sprinkle it with lime, wrap it in plastic and bury it like he had all the others.

Or maybe he could put off the disposal until later this afternoon. He was sort of curious to see what rigor mortis might do. He hadn't had the time or the space to experiment with that sort of thing in the past. His wife before Hillary had made good money, but she'd been on him like white on rice...

If he put off the digging, he could spend the morning watching Evelyn's parents' house. That also encouraged him to wait. According to what he'd read in the paper, Hanover House was scheduled to open in November. That meant he had only a few months to find Evelyn—and to show her that she wouldn't have to worry about moving so far away after all.

✦   ✦   ✦

IT WAS EVELYN'S mother who gave her a ride to the airport. Lara wasn't happy that Evelyn was leaving again. She made that clear with a lecture on how Evelyn should take better care of herself, which Evelyn did her best to tolerate. She'd asked her father to drive her since she'd known Brianne, her younger sister, had to work, but he'd had a tee time that conflicted. To be helpful, he'd lined up Lara, and once her mother had agreed, Evelyn didn't feel as if she could change her mind and take her own car. That would not go over well after the difficulty they'd had getting along on their trip to San Francisco.

"You still have stitches in your head," Lara complained as they reached Logan Airport.

"They won't be there long," Evelyn responded, watching the signs for the various airlines slip past.

"Do you know a doctor in Hilltop? Who will take them out?"

Evelyn shrugged. "Maybe I'll do it myself. It can't be hard."

Her mother shot her a dirty look.

"Okay, I'll drive to Anchorage and have a professional do it."

At last, they reached the drop off and Lara pulled to the curb so Evelyn could get out.

Claiming she was going to miss her flight if she didn't hurry, she said a quick goodbye and grabbed her luggage.

She'd rushed off so fast she thought she'd forgotten something when Lara called before she could get on the plane.

"Mom?" She stepped out of the boarding line so that she wouldn't hold anyone up. "Don't tell me I dropped something in your car."

"No, nothing like that."

"And you haven't run out of gas..."

"Of course not. Your father would never allow me to take the car if it didn't already have gas."

"Then what's wrong?"

"Maybe nothing. It's just that...some guy honked at me a few seconds ago, and when I looked over, he flipped me off."

Evelyn wasn't sure how to respond to this. Her mother wasn't that great of a driver. She drove too slow or changed lanes at the worst possible moment, so Evelyn could understand someone getting frustrated enough to make a crude hand gesture. "Did you cut him off?"

"No! I didn't do anything! I was driving along in my own lane when he came up on the side of me. And it wasn't as if he was angry. He was grinning like...like he knew me and was excited to see me again."

A smile didn't sound in keeping with the road rage her mother normally inspired. "But you didn't know *him*."

"I've never seen him before in my life."

"So...why do you think he did that?"

"I have no idea."

A woman's voice came over the intercom. "This is the final boarding call for Alaska Air flight number 1261 to Anchorage..."

Evelyn was out of time. She had to go. "It could be that he thought you were someone else, someone with whom he might joke around. Maybe he was trying to be funny."

"I guess," she said.

Evelyn pictured the worried face that would go with that voice. "Where is he now? Can you see him?"

"No. He sped away."

Then it had to be nothing, a simple case of mistaken

identity. None of the psychopaths she'd worked with over the years knew her mother. They didn't live in the same place they had when she was attacked, and they kept their number unlisted. It would be difficult for anyone to find them, especially randomly, on the road, but if someone *was* targeting Lara for nefarious purposes, he'd remain in the vicinity, most likely follow her. "Just keep an eye on your rearview mirror, be aware of what's around you at all times, and keep your phone handy," she said. "If you see him again, call the police. It's better to be wrong and safe than right and sorry."

"Okay," she said.

All the other people on the flight had boarded and the attendants were getting ready to close up the plane. "I've gotta go," Evelyn said. "I love you." Then she sighed and turned off her phone. Since Hilltop didn't have cell service, she wouldn't be able to use it much in Alaska, not once she left Anchorage.

But she'd had her landline installed at the bungalow, she reminded herself. She could check in on her mother that way.

✦   ✦   ✦

THE SURGERY HAD paid off. Lara hadn't even recognized him. When he'd honked and given her the finger, she'd looked over at him, completely baffled. It was about the funniest thing he'd ever seen.

Everything else had paid off, too, "Andy" decided.

He'd stayed away from Evelyn and her family for twenty excruciatingly long years and, in that time, he'd carefully set up the perfect cover, complete with a wife who supported him financially and step-kids who made him look no different than any other family man. And now his patience and planning were going to bring him exactly what he'd craved since he was seventeen. He'd found Evelyn. He'd finally fucking found her, just like he'd always dreamed!

Suddenly, Andy could've kissed his latest victim, whether she was dead or not. If she hadn't croaked, he wouldn't have gone to Evelyn's parents' house quite so early. He wouldn't have been sitting there when her mother came out. He wouldn't have been driving behind Lara when she traveled to the gated condo complex where Evelyn must live.

He'd stayed outside the gate, hadn't dared push his luck *that* far. But he'd made a note of the unit Lara had gone to, and he'd seen Evelyn in the passenger seat when they passed him.

He couldn't believe it. He'd been within fifty feet of her. It was almost too good to be true, seemed like just another of the many fantasies he created around her. But it wasn't. This time it was real. And she'd looked so beautiful, like she did on TV.

He couldn't *wait* until he could get close enough to touch her...

That was coming, he promised himself. They'd driven to the airport, where Evelyn had stepped out. It was obvious she was leaving Boston. But that didn't scare him. Her parting with her mother hadn't been an emotional one, so he doubted she'd be gone long. And now that he knew where she lived, he could be waiting for her when she got back.

Or...maybe he'd go after her. She'd been dropped off at Alaska Air. He could easily guess where she was going—off to babysit her new "facility," as he'd heard her call it on TV, currently being built an hour from Anchorage.

Such a remote setting offered so many possibilities, so much privacy and space. He could tell anyone who asked that he was an author, writing a book on the criminal justice system. With the interest Hanover House had been receiving, no one would even question it. He was too good of a liar. And if he was working for himself there'd be no way for someone to check his credentials, even if they *did* question his story.

It was brilliant. And there was one more thing. If he went to Alaska, he wouldn't have to come home to Hillary at night, which was a bonus. He'd be alone with Evelyn until he had his fill...

He adjusted himself. *Now* he was getting excited. He just needed to devise a lie convincing enough to get his wife to buy him a plane ticket to California. His parents would give him money once he got there; they always did. And that would enable him to fly to Alaska.

Imagine the fun he could have with Evelyn if time wasn't an issue...

Chapter 5

FORTUNATELY, EVELYN HAD slept for most of the ten hours she'd been on the plane. Without her mother sitting next to her, brooding, it'd been a lot easier to relax.

After she reached Ted Stevens International Airport in Anchorage, she had to grab a bite to eat, rent a car and drive an hour to Hilltop—and yet, because of the time difference, she arrived before nine-thirty, when the sun was just setting. In June, on the longest day of the year, Anchorage received twenty-two hours of sunlight. But from the beginning of August to the end, the days grew rapidly shorter—by almost three hours.

Evelyn had yet to visit Alaska in mid-winter. There'd been no reason to brave the weather. It wasn't as if she needed to decide whether she'd be willing to come; she knew she'd go wherever the government built her a facility. She'd heard a great deal about the prevailing darkness, however, and wasn't looking forward to it.

She called Amarok as soon as she spotted the straggle of buildings that constituted Hilltop from the ridge above, and asked him to meet her out at Hanover

House, which was ten minutes on the far side of the valley. He agreed, but she beat him there, and she was glad. It gave her an opportunity to stand alone in the dwindling sunlight—before she had to view the damage he'd told her about—and admire the huge stone edifice where she would soon be spending the bulk of her time. Her dream was becoming a reality; this proved it. Fortunately, she couldn't see any graffiti on the front. The portable toilets weren't here, either. She could only guess all of that was inside or in the back.

Maybe the people of Hilltop had room to complain about the type of men she'd be bringing to the area, she thought, but they couldn't say anything about the beauty of the facility itself. The old-world architecture of Hanover House made it look as if it would stand for centuries, like a castle. There were no gargoyles or gothic embellishments, thank goodness, but the lines were a bit Draconian—something others had noticed, too. She'd seen one cartoon that depicted HH as a medieval torture chamber. She'd been lampooned in the same cartoon as the "mad scientist" who was "turning the screws" on the "poor, unfortunate souls" who fell within her power, which was frustrating. If the general populace only knew how well she tried to treat the men she studied, they could never make such an imaginative leap.

She heard a vehicle pull into the lot behind her and turned to see Amarok get out of his government-issued 4x4, which sported a winch and a snowplow. When she saw that he was dressed casually in a flannel shirt and a pair of worn jeans instead of his uniform, she realized that she'd probably pulled him out of whatever he did for enjoyment on a Friday night.

"I'm sorry, I—if you were busy, you should've said something," she told him as he came toward her with that long, confident stride of his. "This could've waited until tomorrow."

His lips twisted slightly. "Don't tell me you're surprised that other people don't work twenty-four hours a day."

She couldn't help noting the sarcasm and feeling slightly defensive at the implication. "I don't work twenty-four hours a day."

He cocked an eyebrow as if he'd refute that statement, so she glanced away to remove the challenge. That was an argument she'd most assuredly lose. "I agree I work too much," she admitted, "but there's no need to exaggerate my hours to *that* degree."

"From what I've seen, if you're not working, you're thinking about work. It's sort of one and the same."

"Excuse me?" she said. "You don't even know me."

He ignored her response. "What happened to your head?" he asked, indicating her stitches. "Were you in an accident?"

"Not exactly."

"I'm guessing it wasn't a bar fight, since I can't see you even going into a bar."

She folded her arms. "It was more like a prison

fight."

"You got into it with an inmate?"

"I was blindsided. Nothing I could do about it."

His eyes slid down to the scar on her neck. "By one of the nut jobs you work with?"

"He isn't a nut job. He knew exactly what he was doing."

He scratched his neck. "You're saying you were attacked. *Again*."

She shrugged as if it hadn't been a big deal, even though it sort of was. "Goes with the territory."

With a shake of his head—in disgust?—he rested his hands on his lean hips. "God, no wonder you hate men."

"I don't hate men," she argued. "You've just decided that you don't like me because you don't like what I'm doing."

"I never said it was personal." He gestured toward the building. "And I'm not the one who tore out the copper here and broke the windows, no matter what you think."

"I would hope not, since you're all I've got to rely on as far as bringing those who did it to justice." Although there wasn't any snow on the ground, the temperature was dropping significantly with nightfall. She buttoned her suit jacket to ward off the chill. "Anyway, you didn't have to meet me *tonight*. You could've put it off."

He shrugged. "I figured I might as well get it over with."

Feeling rumpled after traveling for so long, she wished they *had* agreed to meet in the morning. She was worried about the extent of the damage, was eager to see it in case the reality might offset some of the worry, but she couldn't deny possessing a certain amount of female vanity. She wanted Amarok to think she was pretty, and she could've made a better showing—but that was something she hadn't been willing to kowtow to, hadn't wanted to acknowledge.

It was harder to be so cavalier, however, now that they were face to face. "I'll be quick so that you can get back to...to enjoying your evening, then." She gestured toward the entrance. "Where's the damage? I suppose it's inside?"

"It's everywhere. You just can't see it from the front. No doubt whoever did it was afraid they'd be spotted if someone pulled in—from the construction crew or whatever."

"Have you spoken to the construction crew? Did any of them see anyone they didn't recognize, or anyone who was acting unusual?"

"'Fraid not. Every single one claims everything was fine when they finished up for the night on Wednesday. Thursday morning they arrived to discover the damage."

"And called you."

He dipped his head in response.

"Where's the copper?"

"It was piled in back, but I had them take it inside.

With all the windows broken in the office section, and no real divide between that and the prison section at the moment, 'inside' provides little protection, but...I figured it was better than doing nothing."

Evelyn frowned as they entered what was finished of Hanover House so far. "Do you think they were planning to come back and pick it up?"

"If so, they haven't. I hung out here for quite a while last night, hoping they would."

"That was nice of you," she said.

He caught and held her gaze even though she was reluctant to let him. "I'll take that as your apology for accusing me in the first place."

"I didn't *accuse* you." She lifted her chin in umbrage. "I just... I know how you feel about this place."

"Because I've made it no secret," he said pointedly. "But I'm not dumb enough to come out in open opposition and *then* sabotage the construction."

Evelyn had been prepared for some damage but what she saw proved even more disheartening than she'd expected. He'd been right about the "c" word. The construction crew had focused on trying to get some of the plumbing back in and had left the more superficial damage for later, which meant the graffiti was right there for her to read. "Apparently, someone feels very strongly that I should die." She forced a smile with that statement as if it didn't bother her, but he hesitated as if he could tell it did.

"I'm hoping that's a figurative statement," he said at

length.

"Even if it isn't, they'll have to get in line." Her heels clicked on the concrete as they walked through the facility.

"This makes me sick," she said when they'd toured it all. "It's such a waste to deface property like this. I worked so hard to get the money necessary to build this institution in the first place."

He said nothing, just leaned against some 2x4's that would soon be walls, and watched as she made a note of everything.

"Do you think it'll be reported in the news?" she asked.

"Depends on who the construction workers tell. They're from Anchorage, which isn't ideal if you'd rather keep it quiet. *I* haven't told anyone."

She sighed as she turned to face him. "I can't have this type of thing continue."

"You're going to hire a security guard, aren't you?"

"Yes, but there's not a lot of money left in the budget, especially now that we need to absorb *this*."

He kicked a small piece of scrap wood across the room like a pebble. "From my perspective, you can't afford *not* to have a guard."

"But I'm not even sure it'll solve the problem," she said, watching the piece of wood until it came to rest. "The duration of the job will be too short to attract someone who doesn't already live here. And if I hire someone who's local, it's possible he won't be any more excited to have Hanover House in Hilltop than the person or people who did this. For all I know, I could wind up hiring the culprit."

Amarok shoved off the studs and came toward her. "Have you ever heard the saying, 'You can trap more flies with honey than vinegar?'"

"Of course." She took a step back. "But how does that apply here?"

He held up, but to a certain extent, the size of him still intimidated her. "I suggest you try a different approach, one where you establish a rapport with the community, show them you're not what you appear to be."

She smoothed her wrinkled suit. "You're implying that I appear to be...what?"

"Aloof. An uptight outsider."

He smelled good, but she didn't really want to notice that—or the way his dark hair fell across his forehead with a slight curl on the ends. He needed a haircut, and yet she liked his hair exactly as it is, sort of unruly. He was different than any cop she'd ever met, she decided—different than any man she'd ever met. "I have a Boston accent. I can't overcome the outsider part."

"You could relax, be friendlier."

"I've been friendly!" she argued, stung that he would suggest otherwise.

He ducked his head to peer into her face. "To the mayor and the city council, maybe."

"I haven't had the chance to get to know anyone else," she said, lifting her hands in exasperation.

"Because you haven't created the opportunity."

"And how do I do that? Go knock on everyone's door and introduce myself?" She struck a prayer-like pose. "Ask if I could please join the community?"

"You wouldn't have to go that far. All you'd have to do is come down to The Moosehead now and then, give folks a chance to speak to you."

She shoved the strap of her purse higher on her shoulder. "You really think that would help?"

"I do. Everyone's curious about you, what you're doing here, whether it's going to work out and how it'll impact their lives. They've seen you on TV and they've seen you around town, here and there, getting gas or groceries. But you're largely a mystery. And people are often afraid of the unfamiliar." He looked around. "Maybe the vandalism is a result of that fear and you could make it go away by offering a little reassurance."

That actually made sense. She'd been so busy, so focused, she hadn't even considered that she might be able to change the way she was perceived here, might be able to smooth the path for her move to Hilltop. "But The Moosehead's a bar, isn't it?"

At the uncertainty in her voice, he shook his head. "Forget it. There's no helping you."

"*What*?"

"If you don't want the folks around here to feel as if you're looking down on them, you can't act too good for

The Moosehead. It's where they go every weekend, how they socialize."

"I'm not looking down on The Moosehead. I don't go to bars because it's like...false advertising."

"False advertising?" he echoed.

She could tell she'd caught his interest. "Nightclubs are where people go to find...other people."

"Yeah, like *friends*. That's what I'm talking about."

"If you've seen me on TV, then you know my history. It's not *friends* I'm worried about." She started scooting the trash on the ground around her into a small pile with one foot. "I don't do well with any...sexual interest. So why go out dancing? That's like putting goods on display that aren't for sale."

When she risked a glance at his face, she saw that he was frowning. "Then you're not over it," he said softly.

She could tell he was talking about Jasper's attack. "Of course I'm over it. I'm as over it as I'm going to get, anyway. I'll just...never be able to participate in certain...*things*, that's all."

"Like...?"

"Dancing. Making out." She cleared her throat as if there was more but she didn't continue.

"And...?"

When she gave him a pointed look instead of answering, she could tell he understood that sex was also on the list, but he didn't seem as put off as she expected.

"What if you had a police escort?" he asked. "What if I'd be there tonight to look after you? And what if I promised—*gave you my word*—that I wouldn't let anything bad happen to you? Would you be able to trust me? To unwind a bit? Maybe have a few drinks and make yourself accessible?"

Everyone loved Amarok. He commanded a great deal of respect in Hilltop. That he was offering to be her liaison with the community might make a big difference. Maybe, with his help, she could build a bridge...

"I think so," she said, but she couldn't help envisioning the dark, smoky atmosphere, the smell of alcohol and the close press of bodies on the dance floor, where it would be so easy to get groped. It made her nervous. She didn't know anyone here, not really. She didn't even know Amarok. And yet...she felt she could trust him. "Just...I didn't have time to mess with getting my gun on the plane, so...you-you can't leave me there alone. You have to keep your word."

"I always keep my word," he said. "I'll be your designated driver, see that you get home safely."

She bit her lip as she stared at all the hateful messages that'd been spray-painted on the walls.

"Go back to Boston."

"Pretentious bitch."

"You're not gonna change our town."

And those were the nice ones, the ones without so much profanity.

She drew a deep breath. "Then, sure. Why not? I can do it."

A puzzled expression claimed his face. "You're

acting as if you're about to step into a boxing ring where you'll get your ass kicked. Is it going to be *that* difficult for you?"

She straightened her jacket. "No."

"Great. Let's go," he said, but she stopped him.

"Wait. Do I look okay? I've been on a plane all day. Maybe I should find a mirror—"

"All you need to do is change. Do you have anything that makes you look more...approachable than that suit?"

She gazed down at her clothes. "You don't like what I'm wearing?"

"In case you haven't noticed, no one in Hilltop wears a suit—especially to the bar on a Friday night."

Her mind raced through what she'd put in her suitcase: two more suits and a pair of sweats for when she was alone and hanging out at her bungalow. "I don't have anything that might be appropriate," she admitted.

"You don't have a pair of jeans?"

"Not...not with me."

He rolled his eyes as if he'd never met anyone quite so socially deficient. And he probably hadn't. What'd happened to her at sixteen had ruined her ability to form meaningful connections with other people. Since she'd lost her best friends—in the worst possible way—she'd been afraid to get too close to anyone else for fear that person would somehow be taken from her too.

She didn't care to suffer more loss. It was easier to devote herself to her work and find meaning and purpose there. So she didn't have "friends"; she had "professional associates." And she didn't buy a lot of casual clothing—other than the sweats she wore when she was home alone—because she rarely went anywhere that required jeans and blouses.

"Then we'll make do with what you've got," he said. "But once we get inside, where it's warm, at least lose the jacket."

"Okay," she said and followed him back to town.

Chapter 6

AMAROK SAT AT the bar with Evelyn and bought her a drink. He wasn't sure why he was trying to help her mitigate the hostility the folks in Hilltop felt toward her. He was pissed that she'd managed to get that monstrosity of a prison built so close to his town. But, from the news reports, he had a small inkling of what she'd been through in the past. He felt bad about that. And, if he was being honest, there was just...something about her—besides the fact that she was beautiful. When she quit acting so formal and let down her guard, just a little because it never went down much, it was almost as if he could see the sixteen year old girl who'd been so terribly hurt staring back at him...

That made him angry. Protective.

She'd essentially admitted that she couldn't make love, which was a damn shame. Not only was she beautiful, she was smart, accomplished, dynamic. And now that she'd had a drink and was laughing and talking more freely, he was starting to like her—probably more than he cared to. It wasn't fair that she would be denied such an important and fulfilling part of life.

"So this is the best you can do?" She was talking to Shorty, who owned The Moosehead and had just handed her a new drink. A small, wiry man in his late fifties, he was one of Amarok's favorite people and had been since Amarok was a kid. He'd started flirting with Evelyn the moment she sat down, but he was going about it so outrageously that Amarok could tell she wasn't feeling threatened.

"A drink doesn't get any better," Shorty insisted.

"I'll decide that for myself once I taste it," she teased and nudged Amarok. "What do you think? Do *you* like it?"

"I think he just made it up," Amarok said. "Because I've never heard of a Wild Bill."

"Then you have to try it." She held out her glass to him, something he was fairly certain a completely sober Evelyn would not have done.

He took a sip. "Can't say as it does much for me. I prefer a decent beer."

She finally sampled it herself. "I like it," she said. "I like it a lot."

As the night progressed, various townspeople came over and Amarok introduced her. Most nodded politely, then watched her with a wary reserve. But the more she drank and opened up, the more they did the same.

Before too long she seemed to be having a great time. Amarok got the impression she hardly ever let go, that this was an unusual but much-needed release, and was glad he'd brought her—until Ken Keterwee, who owned a well-drilling and septic tank business, asked her to dance. Amarok had seen him standing off to one side, trying to screw up the courage, and had planned to head him off before he could reach her. But Ken, a big, barrel-chested man of about forty, with hands the size of bear paws, had made his move while Amarok was distracted by something Shorty had said. So Amarok was a little late when he jumped in.

"Not tonight, Ken," he said.

"I wasn't asking *you*," Ken joked.

Before Amarok could reinforce his "no," Evelyn got off her stool. The stubborn smile she wore let him know she was determined to rise to the challenge he'd given her by bringing her here.

"It's okay," she said. "I-I can dance."

She'd told him she couldn't, so Amarok knew she'd feel more secure staying with him, here at the bar. The floor was fairly crowded, which meant she'd get jostled, and once Ken and some of the other guys got a few drinks in them, they might not think about what she'd been through and how the most innocent physical contact could affect her. At the very least, Ken would probably step on her feet a few times with those big cowboy boots of his. "Maybe you can get on the floor next time you come here for a drink," he said to her, but she waved him off and allowed Ken to lead her away.

Because he'd promised to be her designated driver, Amarok limited himself to a single beer as he watched.

She seemed to do fine with Ken. She seemed to do fine when Johnny Milner, a butcher, asked her to dance after, and then Jim Studemeyer, who built cabins and bungalows and had built hers. It wasn't until a slow song came on that she threw him a glance filled with any hint of distress. Then he knew she'd had enough of socializing with her new friends and strode out to rescue her so that she wouldn't have to say no herself.

"Whoa, boys, I bet Evelyn's head is spinning," he said, pulling her away before Ken could get his beefy arms around her. "We'd better let her sit down for a bit."

"What the hell, Amarok?" Ken complained. "I'll buy you a drink if you'll just leave us alone and go back to the bar."

"I am going back to the bar, and I'm taking Evelyn with me," he said. But they'd only gone a few steps when she tugged on his hand.

"Something wrong?" he asked.

She didn't answer. Curving her lips into a sweet smile, she slipped her arms around his neck as if she wanted to dance with *him*.

"You suck," Ken grumbled in his ear as he passed them in search of another partner.

Amarok ignored Ken. At the moment, he had other things on his mind, like how surprised he was that Evelyn had wanted to dance with him when she wouldn't dance with anyone else. "Just say the word when you want to stop," he told her.

"Okay."

They moved in silence for a few seconds. Then she said, "So how am I doing? Do you think they like me?"

He could see a number of men standing along the periphery, waiting impatiently to replace him. "There's no question the men do. I can't imagine their wives will, though."

Her eyes widened. "*What*?"

"Never mind. It was a joke."

"You said they like me, right?" Her head dropped back as she gazed up at him, and he realized by her dreamy expression that she was more inebriated than he'd expected. She hadn't had that much to drink, but she also didn't weigh a lot, and, suddenly, the alcohol seemed to be hitting her hard. "I *told* you I'm not stuck up," she said. "I'm a nice person."

"A nice person who's had enough to drink." He fought the impulse to bring her closer, if only to offer her some support. She was no longer all that steady on her feet. But he made sure they had at least six inches of space between them, in spite of that. "I'm going to have Shorty cut you off."

"Why? I'm not drunk."

"You are *definitely* drunk."

"Maybe I am," she conceded. "But at least I'm more sus-susceptible."

"Susceptible to what?" he asked wryly.

She giggled, which was something else he'd never expected to come out of such a sophisticated woman.

"That wasn't what I meant to say. I mean...*ax...ac-ces-ses-si-ble*."

Even when she found the right word she couldn't say it in her current state. "True. You might be more susceptible, too, but I'm keeping an eye out like I promised," he teased.

Ken flipped him off from a place at the edge of the dance floor where Evelyn wouldn't be able to see him. Amarok offered him a benign smile. Then he glanced down to check on his partner again. He thought she might be growing anxious; they were dancing much closer than before.

But she didn't seem anxious so much as...preoccupied with... his neck? "What are you looking at?" he asked.

She didn't hesitate. "That spot right there beneath your jaw."

"Why?"

"It looks *delicious*."

He stiffened in surprise. Personally, he preferred lips to necks and couldn't help wishing she'd take more of an interest in his. But a neck was about as nonthreatening as a body part could be, so he could understand why she might feel safer admiring an area that couldn't demonstrate any desire.

"That's the booze talking," he said.

"No, it's not." She slanted a flirty gaze up at him. "Even a sober woman would want to taste all that smooth, warm skin, Sergeant."

He told himself to leave that comment right there. She couldn't mean what she'd just said. But then she closed her eyes and ran her nose up under his ear. "And you smell good too."

Amarok's plan to get her to loosen up had worked a little too well. Not only had the alcohol relaxed her, it'd stolen her inhibitions. The buffer of space between them had all but disappeared, to the point that he could feel her breasts smashed up against his chest. They weren't dancing any closer than anyone else, but it felt more provocative—maybe because he knew it was rare that she'd even let a man hold her.

Fortunately for his peace of mind, the song was ending. He figured they'd better sit down as soon as possible, before he had a raging hard on. But she didn't let go of him. She kept her arms locked around his neck and continued to sway against him as if she still heard the music in her head.

She was in her own little world, and yet he could tell she was very aware that he was there with her, especially when he felt her lips brush over that spot under his jaw that had become such a fascination for her. He tried to convince himself that she'd just been turning her head. But he was glad he'd maneuvered them into the shadows, where Ken and the others could no longer see them so clearly when she proved him wrong about that contact being incidental and began kissing his neck in earnest.

The movement of her tongue, and the wetness of it,

turned Amarok's heart into a jackhammer. His natural inclination was to palm the back of her head while he nuzzled her neck in return. But he was afraid if he made *any* move it would spook the hell out her. So he closed his eyes and let her have her fun. After what she'd been through, she deserved to be able to act on the desire she felt. But she evoked such a powerful response in him, it wasn't easy to resist the temptation to show her that a man's touch didn't have to hurt.

He almost slid his hands up her back before he gained control and ordered them to remain at her waist. If he gave her the chance, maybe she'd feel safe enough to invite him to participate, to get him involved. Surely, at some point, even she'd have to admit that it would be more fun...

But the movement of her mouth on his neck was making him rock hard—and he hated to think what would happen if a woman who'd been raped, and at such a young age, felt a boner pressed up against her abdomen. He didn't want her to feel intimidated, rushed or overwhelmed; he hadn't even had a chance to jump in yet. So he put some space between them—but that was all it took to break the spell.

Dropping her hands, she stepped back, as if he'd shoved her away instead of adjusting their respective positions by only a few inches.

"I'm so sorry," she said, looking completely abashed. "I can't believe I did that. I swear I...I thought I was only *thinking* about tasting your neck. I never dreamed I'd really do it."

His skin tingled where her mouth had brought the blood to the surface. "Don't worry," he said. "You owe it to yourself to do something out of character every once in a while."

"But that kind of behavior is...is *sexual harassment*."

He shouldn't have let her have that last drink. How much alcohol had Shorty put in the damn thing? "I think you're getting your words mixed up again. It's *not* sexual harassment. We don't work together. We're just two people dancing at a bar."

Her eyes filled with tears. "We're professional associates! And you're a lot younger than I am, which makes it kind of creepy on top of everything else."

He caught her face, lifting it so that she had to look at him. "*Creepy?* Who gives a shit about the age difference between us? We're both plenty old enough to do what we want."

"No." She shook her head. "I don't know what I was thinking. I was doing good, being nice, dancing with everyone and then"—she seemed to have trouble figuring out how she'd even wound up in his arms—"I guess I went too far in the other direction. All I could think about was you, and the way you look in those jeans, and that smile—God, that smile does crazy things to me."

"If you're trying to turn me on, you're doing a damn fine job," he said.

She scowled. "Don't joke around like that."

He *wasn't* joking!

"What I did is completely *not* acceptable or professional or—"

"Stop making a big deal out of it," he broke in, to let her know she was being ridiculous. He hated the pain he saw in her eyes. In so many words, she'd told him at the prison she was broken. And now she was frustrated that she couldn't seem to get it right even when she tried to be more trusting and friendly. "You're human like the rest of us."

The careless way he spoke finally seemed to get through to her. At least, she managed to gain control of her emotions and stanch the tears that were about to fall. "Right. I'm only human."

Movement in his peripheral vision caused Amarok to look to the side. "Ken's already making his way over," he said. "We'd better go."

"That's a good idea. I need to get some sleep. I'm not thinking straight. I—I'll start over tomorrow."

"You're fine. Everything's fine. Tell him we're leaving. *No more dances with anyone.* Then wait at the bar with Shorty until I come get you."

Her eyes widened. "Where are you going?"

He couldn't tell her the truth, that he needed to give his erection time to go away, so he simply gestured at the restroom.

"Oh." She acted slightly embarrassed that she'd reacted with a bit of panic, but then she grabbed his arm. "You won't leave me here without a way to get home, right? I promise I won't...you know...come on to you again. I'm sobering up."

"For the last time, you didn't do anything wrong. Just wait with Shorty. I'll be right there," he said and turned away. Obviously, she could tell he was shaken up by what'd just happened, but she'd completely misjudged the reason. He could still feel the pull of her mouth at his neck. The memory alone sent a fresh shot of testosterone to his groin. She was starving, he decided. Starving for a little male attention. And he wanted to give it to her.

But he couldn't. That was the very thing that frightened her most.

Once he entered the bathroom, he breathed a sigh of relief to find himself alone. He splashed some cold water on his face. Then he pulled his collar back.

Holy shit. She'd given him a hickey. *Dr.* Evelyn Talbot, the driven but remote, highly educated psychiatrist who was bringing the worst psychopaths in America to Hilltop had put more fire and passion in the way she'd kissed his neck than he'd ever imagined she possessed.

This was the woman he'd heard the mayor call an "ice princess"—and yet she'd just brought him to his knees.

And she'd done it so innocently too.

✦   ✦   ✦

THERE WAS A gun on the nightstand, and it was too big

to be hers.

Squinting to clear her vision, Evelyn leaned up on one elbow to get a better look. Then she fell back because her head felt like it was about to explode. Where was she?

Immediately, visions of the shack where she'd been held captive twenty years ago rose up. Since Jasper had never been caught, the possibility of being taken somewhere similar felt like fate at times.

She was just about to panic when the memory of the night before came tumbling back to her.

She was in Alaska, in her bungalow. She'd gone drinking with Amarok. And then...

She was no longer frightened—she was mortified, because then she'd embarrassed herself by falling all over him on the dance floor, letting him know she wanted him. (Had she really told him he tasted good?) And, as if that wasn't bad enough, she'd thrown up in his truck on the way home, which had to have been such a wonderful way to cap off the evening.

Squeezing her eyes closed, she pulled her extra pillow over her head. She remembered telling him she could let herself into the house, that he should leave, but he wouldn't go. He'd helped her inside, cleaned her up as best he could without actually seeing her naked and put her to bed, which explained why she had towels wrapped around her. He'd been too afraid it would freak her out if he took them off so he could dress her once she'd managed to get her wet clothes off—since he'd put her in the shower with them on.

He'd told her he was going to stay, just to be sure she was okay, but she'd argued with him. In her altered state, she'd needed a gun to feel safe, since she didn't have hers. So he'd finally relinquished his to get her to settle down and sleep.

Was he *still* in the house? He had to be, didn't he? Surely, if he were going to leave, he'd get his gun...

She threw off the pillow she'd used to cover her head. If she had company, she was going to shower so that she could face him with a little dignity. Whatever had possessed her to go to The Moosehead last night, she didn't know. Maybe she'd scored a few points with the locals, but she'd humiliated herself in front of Amarok.

Now she wished she never had to see him again...

"I guess he'll know better than to go drinking with *me*," she muttered.

It wasn't until she was gingerly making her way over to the bathroom that she saw the note on her bedroom door. "Don't shoot me," it said. "I'm one of the good guys."

She chuckled despite her hangover. She was pretty sure he *was* one of the good guys.

But once upon a time, Jasper had seemed like a good guy too.

Chapter 7

AMAROK WAS SACKED out on her couch with nothing but her small lap quilt for a blanket. His head and bare chest stuck out on one end, his bare feet stuck out on the other, but she could tell he was still wearing his jeans. Where he'd put his shirt, she couldn't fathom—it wasn't lying on the floor or the furniture.

But then she remembered. She'd tripped when he was trying to help her into the house, and he'd muttered something about the fact that she already had stitches and swung her up into his arms, which meant he'd gotten vomit on him. He'd taken off his shirt when he'd been trying to clean her up.

Maybe he'd even thrown it away...

Should she go on about her business and let him sleep? Or should she cook him breakfast, apologize for her behavior last night and send him on his way?

She was about to slip out and save herself the humiliation of having to face him. With any luck, they could go the next few months without having to bump into each other. She liked that idea—the idea that maybe he'd forget about the worst of last night, the most embarrassing parts. But he opened those startling blue eyes of his and looked up at her before she could peel her gaze away from the mark she'd left on his neck.

"Hey," he said. "I see you're in another suit. That's a good sign. You must be feeling more like yourself."

"I have a terrible hangover, but I deserve that and more."

He covered a yawn. "I think you got the 'more' part last night."

"True. And, sadly, you paid a price too, even though you were mostly an innocent bystander." She took a deep breath, preparing to deliver the apology she owed him. "I'm really sorry about—"

With a grimace, he lifted a hand. "Please don't apologize *again*. Humans aren't always perfect, Evelyn. I asked you to be real, asked you to come down off your high horse and visit the people of Hilltop where *they* like to hang out. And you did. I respect that and can understand the rest. You don't normally drink, didn't know exactly what was in those fruity concoctions Shorty kept shoving at you, and you wound up overdoing it. It's not a crime."

She liked his dark five o'clock shadow, loved how his hair was going every which way. Somehow seeing him fresh out of "bed" made him even sexier, which was rather...unsettling, since such thoughts were so unusual for her. "Okay, I appreciate your generosity. So why don't I go out and clean your truck, and then we can agree to forget about it?"

"Since I've already cleaned my truck, we can forget

about it even sooner." He gave her a grudging smile. "I didn't think the smell would get better with time."

She returned that smile simply because it was hard not to smile at a man who looked so good. "I can't fault your logic, and of course I'll pay to have it professionally detailed."

"Like I said, I took care of it. It's not the first time I've encountered someone who's gotten sick."

"Well, it's the first time I've ever humiliated myself in that way." And if she had to do such a thing, why couldn't she have done it with someone else?

"I can't say that's anything to pride yourself on," he said. "It's hard to humiliate yourself in front of others if you never hang out with anyone to begin with."

"I have friends!"

"That you go out and have a good time with? Or are we talking about an occasional intellectual discussion—an intellectual discussion about, wait for it, deviant behavior. I'm sure that's *just* what you need. More examples of men who have raped, murdered and maimed."

She fisted her hands on her hips. "I'm not sure you can use last night as an example to show me what I've been missing all these years."

"You could be more cautious next time—now that you're aware of your limits. Most people figure that out when they're teenagers, but..."

"But I didn't go through my teen years the way most everyone else did. Yes, I know."

He tossed her lap quilt aside and sat up. "You did great last night, by the way. Everyone liked you."

She couldn't help feeling gratified by *that* comment. "Do you think I won over the people who damaged Hanover House?"

"Tough to tell, but in this small of a town, I'm sure word will spread that you're not as bad as you seem. It was a step in the right direction."

Although it required some effort, she lifted her eyes from his chest where they tended to drift without her express permission. "Would you like some coffee—and maybe some oatmeal?"

"*Oatmeal?*" He grimaced. "How about eggs and bacon? Or biscuits and gravy?"

"I don't have any eggs and bacon or—or biscuits and gravy."

"Figures. You're even uptight when it comes to food."

She blinked at him. "Is there something wrong with oatmeal?"

"It's just so...healthy." He looked around as if he wanted to put on his shirt but couldn't find it.

"You must've thrown it away," she said.

"*Thrown it away?*"

"Aren't you looking for your shirt?"

"I was. But now that I remember, I put it in the washer along with your jacket."

Her jacket? Oh no! It would be ruined! It needed to be dry-cleaned, but she didn't say anything about that.

"I'll move it to the dryer for you."

"Great. While we wait for it to dry, and you make me that delicious oatmeal you promised, can I use your shower?"

Her heart skipped a beat at the prospect of Amarok stripping off those jeans. He looked amazing in them, but she had no doubt he'd look even better without them—which was another scary thought, at least for her.

"I can let you hold my gun, if it makes you feel any better about allowing a man in your shower," he said when she hesitated.

She laughed. "Stop it. I was drunk when I asked for your gun."

"You didn't just ask for it. You *demanded* it. Wouldn't go to bed without it."

"I can't believe you let me have it! You realize I was *drunk*, right?"

He reached into his pocket and pulled out a handful of bullets. "Exactly why I unloaded it first."

She let her jaw drop in mock outrage. "You gave me a *false* sense of security?"

She thought he might grin. She knew he could tell she was teasing, but he sobered instead. "I wouldn't let anything happen to you."

Her heart began to race for no apparent reason— actually, there was a reason, and she knew what it was, but she wasn't willing to accept it.

She cleared her throat. "Yeah, well, thanks for that, but you should've left. If something like that ever happens again—which it won't—feel free to dump me on the doorstep."

"I promised to take care of you, remember? I would never dump you on the doorstep."

She wasn't sure how to take that statement. To save herself from having to decide, she gestured toward the bathroom. "There's a shower down the hall. Actually, wait. There isn't any soap or shampoo in that one. I haven't stocked it since...well, since there's probably no need to ever stock it. I'll get what you need."

He cut her off before she could reach the hall. "There's no need to move anything. I'll use the one you use."

Acutely aware of how close they were standing, she backed away. "Sure. Okay. Whatever you want."

He didn't move. He just watched her intently.

"What?"

His nostrils flared slightly. "What if I want *you*?" he asked point blank.

Her heart jumped into her throat. She'd assumed they'd attribute what she'd done on the dance floor last night to the alcohol and never mention it again, never refer to the feelings it'd stirred. "Definitely do yourself a favor and look for someone else," she said. "In case you haven't noticed, I'm totally screwed up."

He reached out to take her hand and held it lightly, coaxingly. "You have to get over what happened sometime."

She wished that time was now, that she could bust through the barrier of the trauma she'd been through and finally outdistance those bad memories. Her psychologist, when she'd had one, had encouraged her to "get back on the horse," which was a terrible yet effective cliché for what he'd suggested she do.

But she couldn't risk failing, not with Amarok. She figured she'd embarrassed herself enough where he was concerned.

"I'll have to give it a shot sometime—with someone else," she clarified.

His eyebrows snapped together. "Why someone else? What's wrong with me?"

That mark on his neck reminded her of how wonderful it'd felt to act on the desire he evoked. Even now, her fingers burned to touch his chest, his arms, his flat stomach—maybe more. She couldn't remember a time, not since Jasper, when she'd craved a man like that. "You're too young."

"That's an excuse and you know it. We're both adults."

But a man his age... She couldn't hope to retain his interest for long, even if she could give him everything a normal woman could. That made it sort of pointless to try. "If I ever make love to you I want to be able to do it right," she admitted. If she had to encounter him around town afterward, she'd prefer not to be remembered as the worst lay he ever had.

He let go of her. "You're saying you won't sleep with me because you actually want to? I'm not sure that makes any sense."

She gave him a sad smile. "See?" she said. "And that's just the beginning."

Chapter 8

AMAROK SAT AT his trooper station with Makita, his Alaskan Malamute, at his feet, poring through all the articles he could find on Jasper Moore, the murder of Evelyn's friends and her kidnapping and rape. He'd looked it all up before, when he'd first heard that the government was considering Hilltop for the location of Hanover House, but he'd given it only a cursory read, enough to figure out who she was, why she was coming to town and whether or not he'd approve of her agenda.

He didn't. That hadn't changed. But the level of his personal interest had.

"Beacon Hill Killer Still at Large" was one of the first headlines he came across, which interested him enough to read the article.

> *After brutally murdering three sixteen-year-old girls and attempting to murder a fourth, the Beacon Hill Killer continues to elude police. Jasper Moore, only seventeen, hasn't been seen since a passing motorist spotted Evelyn Talbot nude and bloody and stumbling across the road. She told authorities she'd been held captive and was tortured by her boyfriend for three days in an abandoned shack before he slit her throat, started a fire to destroy the evidence and left.*
>
> *"Someone had to have helped him escape," Evelyn*

Talbot's father, Grant Talbot, told an NBC affiliate this morning. "My wife and I firmly believe that his parents purchased him a plane ticket and got him out of the country as soon as they learned he was wanted by police. A boy his age simply does not have the savvy or the resources to disappear on his own."

Irene Tillabook, principal of the exclusive private school the four victims and the alleged perpetrator attended, disagrees. "The Moores are as heartbroken as everyone else. I've spoken to them. I highly doubt they would protect Jasper in such a way."

"Except that he would likely face life in prison without the possibility of parole if they didn't do *something*," Amarok muttered. That could easily cloud a parent's judgment.

The lead detective in the case was quoted in the next paragraph, saying essentially the same thing. Although he did not formally accuse Mr. and Mrs. Moore, he did say he was "looking into all possibilities," and that included them.

Amarok skimmed the rest of the article, then skipped to the next link.

Ten Years Later—Where is the Beacon Hill Killer?

A boy of only seventeen murdered three female class-mates before the fourth victim got away. And then he disappeared. Where did he go? No one knows. His family claims they haven't seen or heard from him since the night Evelyn Talbot emerged from some trees with her throat slit. Although there have been various leads and "spottings" over the years, none of them have panned out. It seems that Jasper Moore has gotten away with murder.

So what about that fourth victim? Evelyn Talbot finished high school, went on to Harvard and will be graduating this spring with a doctorate in psychiatry. She plans to make the study of violent offenders her life's work, so instead of shying away from the kind of individ-ual who nearly took her life, she will study men who are at least as dangerous in an effort to unlock the secrets of the psychopathic mind.

The heading for the next article read, "Meet Victim Number Four" and was written by a journalist for *The Boston Globe.*

Dr. Evelyn Talbot, a beautiful young woman, sits across from me at a corner coffee shop wearing an elegant, tailored suit. When I called her office, she readily agreed to speak with me because "there needs to be more awareness, more information on how to spot and avoid the dangers psychopaths pose," she said over the phone. This morning she tells me, "The conscienceless live among us. They make up four percent of the population. That means that most people will meet at least one during the course of his or her life. Fortunately, not all of them are serial killers. Some are subclinical and don't kill at all. But they do act in their own self-interest, which means they often get arrested for other crimes, crimes like embezzlement, robbery, assault. Bottom line, they destroy innocent lives, and we need to figure out why they don't possess the same behavioral controls as the rest of us."

After examining the photograph of Evelyn as she'd been that day in the coffee shop, Amarok read the caption: *Evelyn Talbot was kidnapped at sixteen, held in an*

abandoned shack and tortured for three days before her abductor
slit her throat and left her for dead.

He pictured the scar on her neck as he moved on to another article. This one focused on the fact that Evelyn was not abducted and tortured by a stranger. She was nearly killed by the man—or boy since he was only seventeen at the time—that she'd been dating for several months.

"I thought I knew him. I thought he loved me as I loved him," she was quoted as saying. "It wasn't as if I was in the wrong place at the wrong time. I was just living my life as a normal teenager, going to school, attending prom and planning for my senior year, when someone I trusted proved to be very dangerous. Not only did he murder my best friends, he decided, once I saw what he'd done and he couldn't lie his way out of it as he'd initially planned, that I could no longer live, either. Then he'd taken great pleasure in making what he thought were my last days hell on earth."

Never did Evelyn say what kind of torture she'd experienced. Amarok figured that was too gruesome for the papers. But he was curious. *Exactly* what happened in that shack? What had she been forced to endure?

"Bastard," he grumbled as he studied the photograph of Jasper that had been posted in the yearbook that year. From everything Amarok could find, he'd been a popular boy, an intelligent boy, even a talented baseball player. There'd been nothing to warn Evelyn that he might turn on her, which was probably the reason she'd become so obsessed with finding out *why* psychopaths like Jasper did what they did.

Amarok clicked on another link, which gave a little more information on Jasper's wealthy and powerful banker father. Apparently, right after the incident they'd pulled up stakes and moved to California, and every time they were asked after that, they claimed to have had no contact with their son.

Amarok wasn't buying it. Jasper's parents had helped him. They had to have. They claimed he might've killed himself off in the woods somewhere, but if he did that, why hadn't his body been discovered in the past twenty years? Amarok also found it highly suspect that it was his family who put forth the idea, who claimed that he was suicidal. Evelyn insisted on the exact opposite. She said he'd *enjoyed* inflicting pain on her, said that he'd laughed at the people who were searching for her during the time he had her tied up in that old shack.

Makita lifted his head and barked, signaling he had company even before Amarok heard the outer door open. Sometimes in the afternoons, Phil Robbins, who did the cooking at the local diner in the mornings, volunteered to act as a receptionist of sorts in the afternoons. Summers were always busy, what with the influx of hunters and fisherman. But even if Phil was off at the diner by now—it had to be getting to be that time—it was Saturday. He'd be going to Anchorage to visit his mother, so Amarok was on his own.

"Hello?" he called to draw his visitor toward him.

Ken Keterwee stepped into his office and crouched to give Makita, who'd circled around to greet him, a scratch behind the ears.

"Hey," Amarok said. "What's up?"

Ken straightened and hooked his thumbs in the pockets of his jeans. "Saw your truck outside. You're working today, huh?"

"I'm taking care of a few things, yes. What are you doing?"

"Just had some pancakes down at The Dinky Diner."

There weren't many places to eat in Hilltop. Just The Dinky Diner, where Phil worked and Ken had just had breakfast, which was only open until three each day, a drive-in and the limited menu of appetizers and burgers Shorty served at The Moosehead in the evenings. For anything else, folks had to drive to Anchorage.

"Is this about last night?" Amarok asked, since he didn't generally hear from Ken a whole lot.

Ken shifted nervously. "Yeah. I was curious about Evelyn—I mean, Dr. Talbot."

"Curious in what way?" Amarok asked, but he was fairly certain he could guess.

"She isn't nearly as bad as I thought—definitely not the cold bitch everyone has been making her out to be."

Amarok minimized his screen. "Some folks aren't happy about Hanover House. They consider her guilty by association, I guess."

"*You* haven't been happy she was coming to town," he pointed out. "Are you one of those people?"

"I have nothing against her," Amarok clarified.

"So you like her."

"Yeah, I like her."

"But...you're not dating her, are you? Last night it was sort of tough to tell. Sometimes it seemed like you were together, and other times it didn't."

Amarok felt possessive, which was uncharacteristic of him, but he had no claim on Evelyn. "No."

"I didn't think so. In order to have all the schooling she's got, and to have established what she's established in her life, she'd have to be a bit older than you are, right? I'm guessing she's thirty-five or so."

"She's thirty-six." She'd made such a big deal about the age gap between them that it was the first thing Amarok had checked by adding the twenty years it'd been since her "experience" with Jasper to the age she'd been when he did it.

"There you go. I'm thirty-nine, so she's closer to my age than yours. What are you? Twenty-eight?"

"I'm twenty-nine. But what does it matter?"

"It doesn't—unless you're interested in her."

"Even then?"

Ken hesitated. "So *are* you interested in her."

With a sigh, Amarok shoved a hand through his hair. "It won't make any difference no matter who's interested in her, Ken. She's been traumatized. She doesn't even date."

He rubbed his big hands together. "She seemed to enjoy herself last night."

"She was drunk, something she considered embarrassing in the end. I doubt she'll let that happen again."

"So you don't think she'll come back to The Moosehead?"

"I doubt it."

"That's too bad. She's sure beautiful, ain't she?" He whistled. "We don't get many women out here like her. You know...that are so pretty and educated and everything."

"There are plenty of women in Anchorage."

"I guess. If you care to drive there."

Amarok wasn't sure why he'd said that. He didn't go to Anchorage to meet women, either. Maybe he just wanted Ken to do so—and leave Evelyn alone. "You don't happen to know who vandalized Hanover House, do you, Ken?"

He hesitated. Then he said, "It wasn't *me*."

Amarok had never thought it would be. "Then who was it?"

"Don't know," he said, but he sort of mumbled it, which told Amarok he knew more than he was saying.

"You haven't heard anything?"

Ken focused on Makita again. "I can ask around, see what I can find out."

"I've been asking around. No one's talking."

"Because they know you'll have to do something

about it if you catch the guys who are responsible, and I don't think too many people are keen on seeing them punished."

"I can't turn a blind eye when someone breaks the law, Ken. And I'm sure Evelyn would be grateful. She's understandably upset about the damage."

The big man took off his ball cap and scratched his head. "I know. She mentioned it last night. She believes she's going to be able to do so much with that place."

Amarok rocked back in his chair. "It's her hope for making sense of the world, making sense of what happened to her."

Ken rubbed his chin with his thick, callused fingers. "That puts Hanover House in a different perspective, doesn't it?"

"I guess it does," he agreed.

"What kind of man could slit a woman's throat?" Ken asked, crouching to give Makita another pat.

"The kind of men she's bringing to town," Amarok said. "But that doesn't mean I'll tolerate anything that might hurt her or Hanover House. Maybe you should pass the word along."

"I will," Ken said.

"So you're really not going to tell me who did it?" Amarok asked.

Ken's eyes widened. "Come on, Sergeant, I'm no narc. I'm surprised you haven't heard already. They were bragging about it at The Moosehead right after they did it. They thought you'd be *glad* they were fighting back. It wasn't until yesterday, when everyone figured out you *weren't* happy that they clammed up."

"I've never allowed anything like that to go on. What would make folks think I'd start now?"

"Because it was Hanover House! Because you don't want it here, either!"

"We had our chance to stop it. We didn't do enough, and now we have to live with the outcome."

"I understand. And I'll make sure everyone else does, too." He started to go but Amarok called him back.

"It wasn't Chad Jennings and his brother, was it?" Amarok had sort of wondered that from the beginning. They were only nineteen and twenty and wild enough that they were usually to blame for whatever hell-raising went on in Hilltop.

When Ken said nothing, Amarok came to his feet. "Damn it! Their parents have been through enough."

"It's not them," Ken muttered and hurried out.

Although Ken hadn't been very convincing, Amarok couldn't help hoping it wasn't the Jennings boys. There was no way they'd have the money to make restitution. And if they went to jail, it'd be their parents who suffered. Chad and Tex were paying the bills since their mother had been diagnosed with multiple sclerosis and their father had quit his job to take care of her.

With a sigh, Amarok sat down and picked up the phone to call Evelyn. Because so many of Hilltop's residents felt unsure about Hanover House, he thought it would still be wise to hire a security guard for the next few weeks, until the construction crew could get the perimeter fence up and secure the premises. Someone else, someone with more criminal intent than the reckless Jennings boys, could come by for that copper. So he wasn't going to stop her from establishing some security, but he did want to assure her that the vandalism wasn't part of a bigger scheme to make sure Hanover House never opened—and that he'd keep a close eye on the people who might've done it to be sure they weren't stupid enough to do anything like that again.

Chapter 9

SO THIS WAS Hilltop. How was it that Evelyn thought she could tolerate such a place? It wasn't much more than a trading post. And the people! Nothing but stupid hicks.

He was going to have a field day here, "Andy Smith" decided as he cruised slowly down the main drag. It only lasted for a few blocks. Then he had to turn his rental car around to drive back the other way. He'd spotted one small motel with a chain of twelve rooms at the far end. It wasn't fancy, but he supposed it sufficed for the hunters and fishermen who came here, so he figured he could get by with it, too. At least there was *some* place to stay. The farther he drove from Anchorage, the more he'd begun to worry that there would be *no* lodgings.

While braking at one of the three intersections that heralded the main crossroads of this remote dot on the map, he took a second to check his reflection in the rearview mirror. It was the first time he'd be putting his new face to the test. Well, he supposed returning to the States fifteen years ago had been one sort of test. And flipping Evelyn's mother off had been another. But instead of mingling with masses of people who may only have seen pictures of his former self on TV or the internet, or flashing his mug to someone in a car, he'd be confronting the one person who knew him better than anyone else. The one person who knew what he was capable of and had lived to tell about it.

Of course, when the time came and he was ready to make his move, he'd wear a ski mask until he could subdue her. These days, he always wore a mask until he'd secured his victim. But he could bump into her by accident before then—maybe at the diner—and he felt certain that if anyone would recognize him despite the surgery, it would be Evelyn.

So coming here raised the stakes considerably. He'd be hiding in plain sight—which was daring but exciting too. He'd been waiting so long to be able to see her up close, to touch her, that he was ready to take the gamble. And he was fairly confident. Not only had the surgeon done his job well, twenty years had passed since they'd been together in that shack. He'd put on a good twenty pounds of muscle and kept his hair dyed brown to cover the blond. The color of his eyes was the only thing he hadn't been able to change—colored contacts looked so ridiculous they drew more attention rather than less, so he didn't bother with them.

Besides, most people had brown eyes. He hardly considered that a distinguishing characteristic.

He rolled down his window to test the air. It had to be in the mid-sixties—a nice day for somewhere

notorious for being cold. He figured he'd check into the
motel using an old ID, from one of his earlier identities.
Then he'd grab a bite to eat. He needed to familiarize
himself with the area, figure out the best places to hide,
should he ever need to hide, and where every road led,
even the nondescript dirt ones. From looking at a map,
he was pretty sure if something went wrong he'd have to
get back to Anchorage in order to have half a chance of
disappearing again, but having only one escape route
wouldn't give him many options. He'd be wise to do
some investigating and open up other possibilities—at
least find a few places where he could hide until he
could use that main road.

Some of the people he passed on the street watched
him drive by. Obviously, they noticed when there was a
stranger in their midst. But he wasn't worried. It was
hunting season, so he doubted his was the only
unfamiliar face. And, thanks to Hanover House, he had
the perfect cover.

He wondered if it might be possible to hold Evelyn
hostage at her own house, if she had one...

Why not? he asked himself. Who would stop him in
this two-bit town? He doubted there was any law
enforcement to speak of. Even if there was, he couldn't
imagine the force would be very well trained, not way
the hell out here. If he could outsmart the best cops in
the lower forty-eight, he doubted Hilltop would have
anything he'd need to be afraid of.

He imagined sitting on Evelyn's couch, waiting for

her to come home late one night, and chuckled.

Wouldn't that be the best?

✦　✦　✦

AMAROK THOUGHT EVELYN might call him to report on whether she'd managed to hire any security at Hanover House. But he didn't hear from her. So he went over to The Moosehead. He was hoping she'd show up, even though he knew it was highly unlikely. She wouldn't go to a bar on her own; she'd told him as much. After last night, she'd probably be even *more* cautious about that than she'd been before. He just didn't have any excuse to drive over to her side of town, which was what he wanted to do, and thought the bar might offer a distraction.

He proved himself right—that she wasn't at The Moosehead. Then he hung out for a while, drank a beer and listened to the music.

"Hey, where's your pretty doc tonight?" Shorty asked when he came to collect Amorak's empty glass. Shorty's sister, who was visiting for the summer, had poured his beer, but she was in the back, probably doing dishes.

"*My* pretty doc?" Amarok said.

"I heard that you two were making out in the corner last night." Shorty leaned over the bar, which wasn't easy for such a small man, and pushed Amarok's collar back by a few inches. "Yep. There's proof."

Amarok fixed his shirt before anyone else could

take notice. "You can't make anything out of a little monkey bite. She was drunk, didn't know what she was doing."

"And yet she remained selective."

"Meaning..."

"She chose you, didn't she? It's not as if she tried to suck on Ken's neck, although he was dying for it."

So he and Evelyn had a physical attraction. That didn't mean it'd go anywhere. Matter of fact, she'd pretty much told him it couldn't. "She might've given Ken a hickey if he'd been dancing with her at that particular moment."

Shorty lowered his voice. "You're saying there's nothing going on between the two of you."

"That's what I'm saying," Amarok said.

The bartender's grin widened. "Ralph Hazard told me earlier that he saw your truck out at the doc's place this morning."

Amarok stiffened. He knew he lived in a small community, and that he stood out because of his job, but this was getting ridiculous. "Doesn't anyone mind their own business anymore?" he asked. "What was Ralph doing way the hell out there?"

"Picking up a couch for sale next door."

Amarok didn't question that; he'd known Ralph his whole life. But what were the chances he'd have reason to be in the area? Evelyn had built on the far side of town, where there were only a handful of people, and very few houses. "She got sick on the ride home," he explained. "I only stayed over to make sure she was going to be okay."

"Of course," Shorty said. "You were just doing your civic duty."

Amarok leaned closer. "Stop with the sarcastic bullshit."

"What sarcastic bullshit? We've all been wondering when you'd meet a woman capable of catching your eye." His grin slanted to one side. "Or, failing anything more serious, putting the rest of you to good use. I know many have tried and failed. Watched it all play out here at the bar. At least now we know it takes a beautiful, whip-smart older woman to get our diligent state trooper excited."

Amarok came to his feet. "For Christ's sake, she's not that much older than me!"

Shorty hooted with laughter. "I thought that might get a rise out of you. You've got it bad." He lifted a warning finger. "But I can't imagine she's going to like it if she ever learns that you're not too keen on her baby."

"Her baby?"

"Hanover House."

"She knows. I haven't kept my feelings on that a secret."

"And now your feelings for her aren't much of a secret, either," he said with another laugh. Then someone called for a shot of tequila and, with a wink, he hurried off.

After that, Amarok wasn't interested in hanging out at The Moosehead. It was always a good place for law enforcement to be. If there were going to be problems after the sun went down, it was generally at the bar, which was why he dropped in most weekends. Typically, he enjoyed that aspect of his job, despite the number of fights he had to break up, but tonight he couldn't quit thinking about Evelyn. So he gave up trying to hold out and drove over to her place, just to make sure she was okay.

Once he parked in front of her house, however, he almost changed his mind. On the drive, he'd told himself there wasn't any reason they couldn't be friends. She'd soon be living in the area; he might as well accept her, get used to having her around for however long she might stay.

But he wasn't really interested in friendship, and he knew she couldn't give him anything else.

"So *why* are you here again?" he mumbled to himself, but he climbed out of his truck anyway.

She was wearing gray sweats when she came to the door. They weren't revealing—not by a long shot—and yet he preferred the way the soft cotton hugged her curves to the harsher lines of the business suits she normally wore.

"Apparently you *do* dress down occasionally," he said.

A few strands had fallen from the messy bun that held the rest of her hair back. He liked that, too.

She tilted her head back to look up at him. "You're not suggesting I should've worn this to The Moose-head..."

"No." It was just nice to meet the woman behind the "tough girl" mask she normally showed the world. She was so defensive—she had good reason to be—but it made him want to peel back the layers until he could get through to the soft part she was trying so hard to protect. "How'd it go today?" he asked. "Did you manage to find someone to stand guard over at HH?"

"I have a couple of possibilities, but I didn't want to hire anyone without getting your opinion first, since you probably know both men."

He found it oddly gratifying that his opinion mattered to her. "Did you call me?" He couldn't imagine she had. Since there was no cell service in Hilltop, he didn't own a smart phone. But until he'd left for The Moosehead, he'd checked the voicemail connected to his land line after every time he went out, just in case. There'd been no word from her.

"No. I got caught up in some psych evals I had to do, and by the time I finished, I was afraid it was too late. I blew your Friday night; I didn't want to ruin your fun on Saturday, too." She gave him a sheepish grin. "Since you're here, however, do you have a minute to come in?"

"Sure."

When she stood back to admit him, he was careful not to touch her as he brushed past, but that wasn't because he didn't want to. He was determined to give her plenty of space. He felt it was important that she come to him—like she had last night.

He just wasn't sure she ever would...

"So who responded to your ad?" he asked. "Who do we have to choose from?"

"Jayden Willoughby."

He'd been crossing her living room, but at this he pivoted to face her. "Jayden hasn't even graduated from high school yet."

"True. He'll be a senior. But he's got two weeks before school starts, and he said he could come out on nights and weekends if I need him longer. The construction crew is there the rest of the time, so that could work."

He did nothing to hide his skepticism. "Is he even eighteen?"

She gestured for him to sit down. "Yes. Had his birthday in June."

"And option number two?" he said as he dropped onto her couch.

"Mason Thornton."

Amarok remained seated but shoved himself forward. "He's an alcoholic!"

"I could tell by the way his hands were shaking. He also volunteered that information, which I respect. He said he's trying to sober up, so I thought giving him some work might help."

She was considering someone who had such an

obvious problem? Amarok shook his head.

"What?" she said.

"You are *so* much kinder than you seem."

"Yeah, well, don't tell anyone. It'll ruin my image." She gestured toward the kitchen. "Would you like a drink?"

"What do you have?"

"Not a lot. Actually, nothing, except milk or water."

He made a face to let her know he wasn't impressed with the selection, and she laughed. "Sorry, I haven't really stocked my fridge or my cupboards, since I won't be here on a permanent basis for another month."

"So what have you eaten today?"

"I had some canned soup earlier."

"What else?"

She shrugged. "A few crackers?"

"That's *it*?"

"Like I said, I don't have a lot in my cupboards, and once I took off my makeup and washed my face, I wasn't about to drive to town. If you're thirsty, water should work."

He got to his feet and pulled out his keys.

"You're leaving?" she said.

"Yes, and you're going with me."

"I just told you—I've already taken off my makeup. I don't want to be seen in town."

"I like the way you look—and nobody else matters."

Her jaw dropped, as if he'd surprised her with that statement. "Okay, but...where are we going?"

"To get a bite to eat, of course."

"This late? There's nothing open!"

"Shorty serves a limited menu. We'll go to the back of The Moosehead, right by the kitchen, and his sister'll grill us a burger." He extended his hand.

She eyed it. "Amarok—"

"Take my hand, Evelyn."

"I can't."

"Sure you can." He ran a finger lightly down her arm. "Going to get a burger with me is harmless."

She looked slightly troubled as she stared up at him. "But what I feel when I look at you isn't."

Carefully, but very obviously, he weaved his fingers through hers. "See? This isn't so bad, is it?" he murmured and felt a certain warmth when she let him lead her from the house.

✦   ✦   ✦

EVELYN PUT HER feet up on the dash of Amarok's truck and stared at the stars beyond his windshield, which were so much more vivid in Alaska than anywhere else. She was fairly certain she'd never tasted anything as good as the bacon and cheddar quarter pounder he'd brought her from Shorty's kitchen—or felt more secure or happy than kicking back with him in the parking lot of The Moosehead, where they could hear the music from inside drifting out onto the cool evening air.

"It's beautiful here," she said. Maybe Hilltop didn't have a lot of other things to recommend it, but it certainly had stunning scenery.

"*I* like it," he responded, following her gaze up into the sky.

"How long have you lived here?"

He was making quick work of his meal, much quicker work than she was. "All my life."

She took another bite of her own burger. "What kind of a nickname is Amarok?"

"It's Inuktitut."

"The language of the Inuit people." She'd read about some of the various Alaskan natives once she'd heard where Hanover House would be located.

"Yes."

She selected one of the crisper French fries from the basket in the seat between them. "What does it mean?"

"Wolf."

"Have you been called that all your life?"

He swallowed the bite he'd taken of his own burger. "For most of it. My friends gave me the nickname after some bully picked a fight with me in grade school."

"You must've won that fight."

"That kid never messed with me again," he said with a cocky grin.

She stuffed another fry into her mouth. "So, let's see...when that was happening to you, I was...what? *In college*?"

He slanted her a look that said he wasn't happy with the topic of conversation. "We're going there, are we?"

"Don't you think we should?"

He scowled. "Definitely not."

"Because?"

"What's the point?" he said with a shrug. "As far as I'm concerned, it doesn't matter."

She sat up. "Of course it matters. Relationships are hard enough when both people are at a similar stage of life. And that's when you're dealing with 'normal' people. We both know I'm not 'normal.'"

"Everyone has their challenges."

She laughed without mirth. "Not many people have *my* challenges. We have too much stacked against us, Amarok." As far as she was concerned, whatever spark they felt they'd be wise to smother right away. It would be far easier to end things now, before either one of them could be hurt—before they could get carried away with hope only to be disappointed by the limitations imposed by her dysfunction.

"That's it, then?" he said.

She was fairly certain he'd never had a woman tell him no, and she could understand why. "Maybe I haven't been clear enough, but"—she lowered her voice even though there wasn't anyone else around to overhear her—"I can't have sex." She figured she might as well be blunt, get it out there. "I'm guessing that'll be important to you."

He wiped his mouth. "Important but not everything."

Her appetite suddenly gone, she put her burger on the wax paper it'd been wrapped in. "You're serious."

"Is that all you think I want?"

She drew a deep breath. "I'm not sure what you want, but I'm pretty sure I can't give it to you, regardless."

He caught her wrist before she could come up with a napkin to wipe the ketchup and grease off her right hand. "I don't believe that," he said and proceeded to lick her fingers clean.

Something deep in her belly reacted so strongly to the sensual nature of what he was doing that Evelyn gasped. It felt like she'd just come screaming over the first hill of a roller coaster.

"See?" He knew she liked it; she could tell by his satisfied expression. "It wouldn't be *all* bad."

She was far more afraid of it being *good*. The physical element was one thing—that was a big challenge. But it was falling in love that terrified her most. Not only had Jasper hurt her body, he'd broken her heart, betrayed her trust and destroyed her confidence.

She pulled her hand away while she still had the will to do so. "It'd be a mistake to even try," she said. "Please, take me home."

He studied her for several long seconds. She could tell he was conflicted, that there were so many things he wanted to say. The obstacles she faced were difficult for someone who'd never been through the same type of trauma to understand. But he didn't attempt to argue with her; he started the truck.

Once they reached her bungalow, Evelyn almost

jumped out before he could come to a complete stop.

"Thanks for dinner," she mumbled.

He caught her arm, then let go right away as if he'd reacted out of instinct but wanted to show her that he would never be forceful with her. "Will you do me one favor?"

Tamping down all the useless desire he evoked, along with the frustration of feeling that desire and not being able to act on it, she swallowed around the lump in her throat. Tears seemed to be her only outlet, but she wanted to get away from him before she broke down, didn't want him to see her cry. "What's that?"

"Just give me a chance," he said softly.

"Isn't it a little premature for...for *this*?" she asked. "You barely know me."

"I figure, in our situation, it's especially important not to play games. I'm putting my heart out there, trying to make it easy for you. That's why I'm telling you so soon. I'll help you get through whatever your issues are. I just need you to try and trust again."

"I'll think about it," she responded and fled.

Chapter 10

IT WASN'T UNTIL Amarok heard the word "vandalism" that he realized Eric Bilichek, a plumber he'd known for years who sat a few seats down from him, and the stranger next to Eric, were talking about Hanover House. Then he couldn't help but eavesdrop, just in case they said something about who had damaged the building. Amarok didn't want to charge the Jennings boys, if they were even to blame. But if they committed the crime, and he had enough evidence to arrest them, he had to do so. He was the law around here, and the law couldn't turn a blind eye no matter the reason *he* might personally want to.

"So who did it?" the stranger asked, holding his morning coffee loosely in his hands.

"No clue." Eric shoved what was left of his breakfast away from him, so that Sandy Ledstetter, the only waitress currently working the bar at The Dinky Diner, could pick it up. "I wouldn't turn the guy in even if I did," Eric added with a humorless chuckle. "He just did what we've all been tempted to do—make our feelings known. But the fact that it happened just goes to show that you're right. Folks here are worried, not sure we should've let Hanover House come to town."

"Can't blame 'em for being skeptical of a place like that," the stranger said. "I mean, who is this chick—Evelyn Talbot? And what does she think she's going to be able to do, anyway?"

Eric wiped his mouth and put his napkin on his plate. "She's supposed to be a pretty good psychiatrist."

"Doesn't matter *how* good she is. Psychiatry in general is a joke—a pseudo-science. No one can figure out what other people are thinking—or control behavior. And having Hanover House here will change the whole community, bring in a lot of outside attention. Is that what folks here want? Did anyone even bother to ask?"

"Some asked, but there aren't a lot of ways to earn a living in such an out-of-the-way place. I think most people decided it could be a blessing to those who need the work."

"A blessing!" he scoffed in disbelief. "You want to know what I bet? I bet before long she'll be pushing the government to expand, maybe even build other facilities here. There's a place in Arizona that has *seven* prisons. Can you believe that? They have more *inmates* than citizens." He shook his head. "Whoever let that happen was crazy."

"One prison is plenty," Eric responded. "We don't want any more."

"Then you're going to have to make sure Dr. Talbot doesn't get her way again. Fight her and everyone who stands behind her. If the people in the lower forty-eight can dump all their human garbage where they no longer have to smell it, they will. And if just *one* of those bastards ever gets loose"—the stranger whistled—"you and everyone else here will be totally fucked. It'll be like shooting fish in a barrel!"

"Not necessarily. Most folks in these parts are armed," Eric said. "I promise you—anyone who comes after me is going to get a bullet between the eyes."

"Easy to say." The man lowered his voice. "But have you ever killed a man?"

Amarok couldn't help leaning forward to get a better look at the stranger's face. He didn't like his tone, or his bravado, either. He also didn't see why someone from outside the area would have such a strong opinion on Hanover House. Why did this jerk care so much?

"Of course I haven't killed a man," Eric said. "But only because I've never had to."

"It takes a certain kind of person," the guy responded.

"Anyone can kill," Eric argued.

"No way. You'll never see it coming. These are hardened murderers we're talking about, people who delight in fear and degradation and pain. There won't be a damn thing you or anyone else can do, least of all Evelyn Talbot. It's not as if she's like some animal trainer who'll have a special rapport with the men she counsels. She'll probably be the first to take it in the ass and then have her head lopped off."

Eric finished his water. "If one escapes, the police

will catch up with him eventually."

"What police? From what I hear, you have only one state trooper in the area—and he isn't even thirty years old."

Eric must've seen Amarok walk into the diner, because he turned and glanced down the bar with a *"I didn't say that,"* kind of look. Eric was familiar with him, but the stranger would have no way of knowing *he* was that state trooper. It was Sunday morning, so he wasn't in uniform.

"Sergeant Amarok's all right," Eric told the guy. "Believe me, what he doesn't have in age, he makes up for in ability. He's been an Alaskan State Trooper for at least eight years, and he's done a damn fine job of it so far."

"A damn fine job of handing out citations for hunting or fishing in the wrong places?" the stranger said. "Or removing animal carcasses from the road?"

Eric cleared his throat. "Maybe you didn't notice me look that way a second ago." Or he didn't care. That was the impression Amarok got. "But that trooper you mentioned? He's sitting right there. And he just heard you."

The stranger leaned forward and met Amarok's gaze, but instead of acting embarrassed or apologetic, he grinned with an insolence that made Amarok want to punch him in the face.

"I was just stating my opinion. That's not a crime, is it, Sergeant?" he called down.

"No, it's not a crime at all," Amarok responded. "What brings you to town?"

"Oh boy. Now he wants to know what I'm doing here, which means I've gotten on his bad side." The stranger's smile widened, as if he was enjoying this exchange. "I'd better be careful not to speed or run a stop sign."

Eric tossed his new "friend" a grimace. "Sorry, Amarok," he said as he laid some bills on the counter. "I barely met this dude, didn't realize he was such a prick," he said and walked out.

The guy's smile didn't waver despite Eric's words. "Oh no. Now I've also offended a friend of yours."

"He merely stated his opinion," Amarok said. "That's not a crime, remember?"

Sandy had started toward them with the coffee pot but, hearing what was going on, she froze. "Excuse me, but we're *all* friends of Amarok's," she said. "So I'd be careful what you say about him."

Laughing softly, the guy came to his feet. "This place is *great*."

After he paid his bill and left, Amarok got up to watch him climb into his car. It was a nondescript, white sedan—a rental car.

Sandy came around the counter to stand next to him.

"Have you ever seen that guy before?" Amarok asked her.

"No. Never."

"Then you don't know his name."

"Actually, I do. Said his name was John. He was flirting with me before you came in. Told me he likes brunettes."

Sandy was only nineteen. "He's a bit older than you, isn't he?" Amarok felt a bit hypocritical pointing that out after protesting the age difference between him and Evelyn, but this was a much wider gap.

"By like twenty years!" she said. "He seems to think a girl like me, stuck out in 'the middle of nowhere,' as he put it, should be happy to catch the attention of a guy like him."

"You didn't accept his offer?"

"No. He's...I don't know. Disrespectful. I'm not interested."

Amarok rested his hands on his hips as "John" paused to wave before pulling out of the lot. "Did he happen to mention his last name?"

"No, but he said if I wanted to have a good time, I could stop by the motel tonight, so that must be where he's staying."

"Good information to have," Amarok said. That meant Margaret Seaver down at The Shady Lady would be able to provide a full name and possibly a home address.

As soon as Amarok arrived at his trooper station, he called Margaret and got the information he wanted. Then he ran it through his computer. If John Hanson was hitting up innocent young girls like Sandy and weighing in on local matters, matters that shouldn't concern him, Amarok figured it might be worth checking to see if he had any outstanding warrants.

But his record was clean. He didn't even have any citations.

"Too bad," Amarok muttered. It would've been an absolute pleasure to arrest him.

✦   ✦   ✦

A SECURITY GUARD came out to meet Jasper almost as soon as he parked in the as yet unpaved lot at Hanover House. It hadn't been hard to find the construction site. When he'd asked what the place looked like, several people had explained how to get to it, and no one seemed to find the fact that he'd be interested odd. Probably because Evelyn's pet project had received so much outside interest already—from job applicants to activists to journalists. On top of that, almost everyone in town was talking about the prison and the vandalism that had occurred recently, so it was top of mind.

Jasper wondered how Evelyn had taken the news that not everyone here would welcome her with open arms. Had that come as a surprise? Or had she already known she wasn't a popular figure?

Did she even care?

Yes. The girl he'd known would care. That was what had fascinated him so much. She cared about everything.

"Excuse me, sir!" The guard was almost jogging in

his hurry to reach Jasper. "This is a construction site. It's not yet open to the public. I'm afraid I'll have to ask you to leave."

The red-nosed man seemed a bit over-zealous about his job. But he was also twitchy, nervous. Or maybe he wasn't nervous so much as he was a drinker, Jasper decided. That made him an odd choice for a security guard, but Jasper supposed he shouldn't be surprised by anything he found out here. The people in Alaska did things a little differently—not to mention there weren't a lot of people in the labor pool to choose from, so maybe whoever had hired him hadn't had much choice.

"Sorry. Didn't mean to alarm you," he said. "Is Dr. Talbot around?"

The guard drew himself up short and calmed down when Jasper pretended to have a legitimate reason to be there. "No, sir. I'm afraid she's not." He lifted a hand to protect his eyes from the sun. "Was she...was she supposed to meet you here?"

"No. I was just hoping that I might be able to catch her." He smiled with confidence. He hadn't expected to encounter a guard, but once he'd seen that someone with a radio had been posted to look out for the development, he couldn't turn around and leave. That would only make his actions more suspicious.

"She was here earlier," the man said. "But she's gone back to her place now. She can't work without internet service, and there's nothing like that out here quite yet."

"Of course not." He stood back to stare up at the building. "Would you look at this place?" he said and part of him was sincere in his admiration. How had the broken girl, the girl he'd left on the dirt floor of that shack with blood pouring from her neck, managed not only to recover but thrive? To bring such a major project to pass?

"It's going to be something," the man agreed.

"It should definitely prove interesting."

The way the guard hooked his thumbs in his pants and stood in a slouch gave Jasper the impression he no longer felt threatened. "Are you one of the psychologists who'll be working with Dr. Talbot?"

"No, I'm a writer. I've read about this place, think I might like to include a bit about it in a book I'm doing on advancements in the criminal justice world. But I haven't yet decided if I'd really call this an 'advancement.'"

The red-nosed man rubbed his face. Then he said, "Because..."

"I'm not quite as convinced as Dr. Talbot is that there's anything anyone can do to curb a man's lust for killing."

The guy blinked in surprise. "Why not?"

"Because everyone's so different. Generalities cause problems whenever they are applied to humans. What may be true about some psychopaths might not be true about others."

"I-I wouldn't know about that," he said.

Convinced that he'd already established a rapport, Jasper studied him. "What's your name?"

"Mason Thornton. And you are?"

"John Hanson. From Texas, most recently."

"It's nice to meet you, sir." The guard accepted his hand and shook it rigorously. "I'm sure Dr. Talbot will be sorry she missed you."

"It's not as if we had an appointment," he said. "I wanted to do a bit of research before contacting Dr. Talbot. But I'm definitely interested enough to speak with her now. Maybe I'll go by her place—if I can find it." He gestured toward the road that'd brought him here. "I know I go out and turn toward Hilltop. Then I make a left at the first road—"

"No, that'd be a right," Mason Thornton corrected. "You go down to the bottom of the hill on Greenscape, make a left on Edison and then, after about five miles, take a right by the big water tower, where you'll find a little street called Great Basin. Turn left there. Her house is the fourth one you'll come across."

"That's it. I guess I got turned around." He smiled pleasantly. "But I'm sure I can find it now. Thank you so much for your help."

"It was my pleasure," Thornton said, and Jasper waved as he walked back to his car.

This was going to be too easy.

Chapter 11

EVELYN ADMITTED SHE *wanted* to sleep with him. That was the part that drove Amarok crazy. She wanted him—and he wanted her. So it seemed as if they should be able to overcome all the rest, no matter what stood between them.

"Dammit," he muttered as he wandered listlessly around his house. It was getting late. He should go to bed. Tomorrow would be the start of another work week. But instead of heading down the hall and peeling off his clothes, he kept eyeing his keys and thinking about the beautiful psychiatrist who was staying for only a short time on the other side of town.

She'd let him get a lot closer to her than anyone else, maybe since Jasper. He liked that she trusted him that much. He also liked the rather shy way she'd let him take her hand before they drove over to get that burger.

But would what they felt go anywhere?

He couldn't remember another woman ever getting under his skin quite like this.

Of course, he'd never met anyone quite like Evelyn Talbot. As much as he disagreed with the risks she took, he had to admit that she was something special, a woman unlike any other.

When his phone rang, he hurried over to grab it, but it wasn't her. Caller ID showed his father's number.

Amarok wasn't eager to talk to Hank. Typically, they got along well. Amarok even liked his stepmother, Joanne, who was a fairly recent addition to his father's life. But the three of them were in the middle of a disagreement over how he should handle his real mother.

Amarok would've let it go to voicemail, except he figured it would give him something to think about besides Evelyn, and that seemed kind of important at the moment. "'Lo?"

"What's going on?" Hank asked.

"Not a lot."

"Prison finished yet?"

"No, and it won't be for a couple of months." He considered telling his father about the vandalism. Hank wasn't the type to blab about it to anyone. Since he'd moved to Anchorage almost as soon as Amarok had become an Alaskan State Trooper, he wasn't all that invested in Hilltop. But Amarok didn't care to talk about anything that reminded him of Evelyn. The idea behind accepting this call was to forget about her for a while.

"Are you still angry it's there?" Hank asked.

"I'm not excited about it." Just the woman behind it...

"So...have you decided?"

Amarok could tell by the tone of Hank's voice that he was changing the topic. "I gave you my answer when we talked last time, Dad."

"I was hoping you'd change your mind."

"No."

"Come on, Amarok. Your mother's specifically requested that you be there, and she's not getting any younger. What's the point of holding a grudge? It's time to forgive her."

Just last week his twin brother, Jason, had called from where he lived in Seattle to say the same thing. "She left me, Dad. She dropped me off at a friend's house, took my brother and moved to Seattle without even telling us. I can't believe *you're* the one who's asking me to forgive her."

"She wasn't happy in Alaska. And since I didn't have the money to go after her, I was just glad she didn't take both of you."

He sank onto one of the chairs at his kitchen table. "She could've called me occasionally. Remained part of my life. But she didn't. She's the one who cut contact, not me."

"But don't you see? That was something else I was grateful for. I didn't want you begging me to leave Hilltop too—to go to your mother and brother."

"So you didn't tell me I had a brother? You let me be blindsided when Jason called me on our eighteenth birthday?"

The phone went silent. Then his father sighed audibly. "I'm sorry for that. I've apologized before. I figured what you didn't know wouldn't hurt you."

"Dad, I love it here. It's in my blood. I'll never leave."

"I understand that now. I wasn't as sure of it then."

"Yeah, well, thanks for the lack of faith."

His father ignored his sarcasm. "Then you won't come to your mother's 50th birthday party? We'll all be there—for the first time in years."

"I won't be there. I don't wish her ill; I just don't care to associate with her."

"All right. I won't ask again," he said. "So, will you be visiting Anchorage any time soon?"

Amarok rubbed his forehead. His father seemed happier than he'd ever been. His seafood exporting business had been picking up, and Joanne treated him a great deal better than his first wife. Amarok was grateful for that, didn't want to ruin it. "I'll come this weekend or the next."

"Great. Let us know what day you pick. We'll make you a nice dinner."

"Thanks," he said. Then he told his father he had to go, that he had to be up early and took Makita outside before heading to bed.

✦   ✦   ✦

EVELYN FELT UNEASY. She wasn't sure why. She supposed she was still getting used to her new home.

She was also beginning to regret building where she had. While the other doctors on her team had chosen to live close together, in a small, rather exclusive enclave north of town, she'd come out this way to take advantage of the view. She'd also wanted some space, the ability to break away from those she worked with, at least at night. But the only neighbor she'd met so far had a mentally handicapped son who stared at her whenever she drove by, without blinking or waving or responding in any way. And that gave her chills, even though she knew it was just her background coming into play. She saw danger lurking around every corner. The mayor and several other people had told her that Kit was harmless and, when she was thinking clearly, she believed it.

Determined not to succumb to the fear that could so easily creep into her consciousness, she tore her gaze away from the darkness behind the edges of the blind that covered her office window and continued to pore over the file she'd been reading on a man by the name of Cary Wolff. Like Jasper, Cary had started killing when he was only in his teens. Unlike Jasper, Cary had been caught and was currently in a Colorado maximum-security prison.

She wanted to add him to the roster for Hanover House, but that meant she'd have to forego another inmate she'd already put on the list. She was just trying to decide which one to replace when a noise from outside brought her head up. It sounded like a vehicle had pulled into her drive, and yet, when she went out into the living room and parted the drapes to look out, she didn't see anyone.

Feeling even more anxious, she dug her cell out of her purse and stared at the "no service" message at the top. She hated that she couldn't use her smartphone in Hilltop. She'd come to rely on it for almost everything, from email to directions to listening to music to reading and watching movies.

At least she had a land line, she told herself. It wasn't as if she was completely cut off.

"Why did the government have to pick *Alaska*?" she mumbled and was about to head back to her study when she spotted a pair of headlights. She might not have thought anything about a car being in the area—she did have a few neighbors—but they were down the street to her right, not her left. Her street turned into a dirt road that led up into the mountains about a mile after her place. Why would anyone be up that direction so late at night?

And it was odd the way they were angling their car, because it made the lights shine right on her house.

Could it be a couple of kids, making out? She could see someone parking on the hill to enjoy the few scattered lights of Hilltop below. But why would they park in such a strange fashion—and why wouldn't they turn off their lights?

Once again, she wished she'd brought her gun, knew she'd feel safer if she had it. But she'd been in too much of a hurry. When she traveled with it, she had to disclose that she had one even though she always checked it with her baggage, and that extended the time it took to get through security, because they had to search her bag to make sure it was in a locked case and that she'd conformed to their other rules and regulations.

For this trip, she hadn't been planning to be gone long, had figured the chances of anything happening to her while she was here had to be minimal. None of the psychopaths she was bringing to town had been moved yet, and Hilltop hadn't had a murder or anything like it in years.

Now she felt as if letting those practical concerns overcome her usual caution had been a mistake, however. Staring back at those headlights gave her the creeps. What was that person—or people—doing? Why were they there?

She thought of Amarok, wanted to call him. She'd wanted to call him all night, but now she felt as if she might be justified. Like she'd told her mother, it was better to be safe and wrong than not safe and sorry.

After staring at those headlights for another several seconds, during which that vehicle didn't move, she hurried over to her phone.

But when she lifted the receiver, she couldn't get a dial tone.

✦ ✦ ✦

JASPER PUT ON the backpack he'd prepared in Anchorage. Then he pulled on his ski mask. There wasn't anyone around, but in case the worst happened, he didn't need someone who knew what he looked like these days helping the police build a composite sketch, and he sure as hell didn't care to set himself up for more surgery. With all the empathy his parents felt for others, they wouldn't be able to justify helping him if they learned that he'd killed again. They'd only done it the first time because he'd told them he was high on acid when he killed Evelyn's friends and thought they were zombies—and then Evelyn had surprised him, and he'd panicked.

No, it was far more practical to protect his identity, to mitigate the risk. Although at first, he'd hated having to wear a mask, he'd used it so much in the past twenty years that it had become part of the fun. Feeling the heat of it, the scratchy fibers against his cheeks, signaled to his brain that he was about to engage in what he loved most.

That excitement nearly consumed him now. He wasn't going out to kidnap another woman who *looked* like Evelyn; he was going to confront Evelyn herself.

He'd parked his car such that he'd been able to shine his lights on her house long enough to let her know *something* terrible was about to happen. He liked the idea of giving her a good scare, of making her wonder if her day of reckoning had come. Invoking that kind of terror was an important part of the foreplay, and he'd always been good at foreplay.

Since then he'd moved his rental car down the windy street and parked it off the road behind some trees. He was a stranger in the area. He didn't want anyone else to spot it. The more careful he was, the less likely it would be that he'd have to answer for this later—and what good would it do to finally finish off Evelyn if he went to prison for it?

Careful not to make a sound, he crept around to the far side of the bungalow. He wasn't concerned that she would figure out he was about to break in. She couldn't get away, regardless. She couldn't even call for help, since he'd cut her phone line. He was only being so quiet because he wanted to check things out before he made his move. He'd be a fool to underestimate her: She could be armed.

If he could get another glimpse of her, it would help him know if she was carrying a weapon, he thought, as he moved silently from window to window...

But she wasn't in the living room anymore, where he'd briefly caught sight of her from the car. And he couldn't tell if she was in the bedroom. There were blinds instead of drapes in the bedroom, and those blinds were down.

"Where are you, Evelyn?" he breathed to himself and paused to listen. He even put his ear to the back door.

Nothing.

He figured he might as well break a window. Someone with her background would have deadbolts on all the doors, so he doubted he'd be able to kick one in.

Closing his eyes, he reveled in a rush of anticipation while imagining how the next few seconds would go. If she had a gun, the noise he was about to make would most likely draw her to him—and he'd have to make sure, if she fired, that she missed. If she didn't have a gun, she'd probably try to run.

Either way, he'd have to move quickly to subdue her. But she'd be scared shitless. She'd have to be. And there was nothing more debilitating than fear. He'd seen it so many times: people who could usually think and act quite rationally freezing up in terror. Since Evelyn, of all people, would have a clear knowledge of what was in store for her, he didn't think it would be hard to gain the advantage. Even if she had a gun, she'd be lucky to get off one shot, which would probably go into a wall or the ceiling, before he could shove the barrel of his own firearm in her mouth.

He was fairly certain *that* would put an end to all resistance. Then he could put the gun in other orifices—and with someone as strong as Evelyn, the torture could last for days.

It had before, hadn't it?

Choosing the widest window, he pulled out the small area rug he'd shoved in his backpack. It was thick enough to protect him from the broken glass, thicker than a blanket or a towel. But before he could lift the butt of his rifle, he heard the sound of a vehicle coming

down the street. Then a car door slammed, a dog
barked, and, almost right after, someone rang the
doorbell.

Chapter 12

"WERE YOU THE one sitting down the street?" After checking the peephole, Evelyn had opened her front door to find Amarok, and the beautiful Alaskan Malamute she'd occasionally seen with him in town, standing on her front stoop.

Amarok seemed taken aback. "Sitting down the street?"

Pressing a hand to her chest in an effort to slow her heartbeat, Evelyn leaned out of her house to be able to see where that car had been. It wasn't there any more. It had driven away ten or fifteen minutes earlier. She'd definitely taken note of that. But the memory alone made her uneasy. "Someone was parked right there." She pointed to the spot. "They stayed for several minutes, but...I'm pretty sure it was a car, not a truck."

"It wasn't me," he said. "Did you happen to get the make and model of the vehicle?"

"No. It had its headlights shining right on the front of my house. I couldn't see anything for the glare."

"When I was driving here, I didn't pass anyone on *this* street." He looked at her with concern, as if he could tell she was badly shaken. "Are you okay? Did whoever was driving that car threaten you in any way?"

She shook her head. "No. To my knowledge, they didn't even come on to the property. But...my phone's dead, which seemed significant, since there's been no storm, no reason for it to go out—especially at the same time I have someone shining their lights into my house so late at night."

He glanced up and down the street, which was perfectly dark and quiet. "Go back in and lock the door," he said. "I'll take a look around."

She caught his arm. "Wait. How did you know?"

"How did I know what?"

"How did you know to come?"

"I didn't," he replied.

"So why are you here?"

When he paused, she didn't think he was going to answer. But then he lifted her chin with one finger. "I wanted to see you before you left. I was afraid you'd go back to Boston in the morning and decide"—he shook his head as if he wasn't convinced he should continue, but he did—"decide to carry on as usual, without giving me another thought."

She didn't know how to respond to that. What she wanted and what she could allow were two different things. But she was glad he'd shown up when he did. She'd had herself talked into all kinds of craziness—that Jasper had finally caught up with her, or one of the psychopaths she'd evaluated over the years had come to kill her. Even with her phone out, that seemed like an overreaction now, but it'd felt incredibly real a few seconds earlier.

When she slipped her arms around Amarok's neck, she could feel his surprise. But then his hands slid up her back, and he held her against him. She needed the embrace, needed his warmth and the reassuring firmness of his body to help her stop shaking.

"It's okay," he whispered as his lips brushed the temple that didn't have stitches. "I'm sorry you were frightened. But nothing bad's going to happen. I promise."

The problem was...she knew that something bad could *always* happen. "My phone's out," she said, going back to that. "Why would my phone be out unless—"

"Don't assume the worst," he broke in. "I'll check it, see what's going on. But even if someone cut the line, what you've been through is no secret. Whoever did it could simply be trying to scare you."

They'd succeeded. It didn't take much. Although she hated to admit it, those scars—the ones on the inside—made her so vulnerable. She'd probably always be easy to spook. A lot of times, even when she had her gun with her, she would lay awake at night, listening to every sound. "You think someone wants to scare me away from Hilltop? That it might be...might be the same person who vandalized Hanover House?"

"That, or it's possible someone just thinks it's funny. But if I find out who that someone is, I'm going to make them awfully sorry." He stepped back and told his dog to go inside with her. "Makita will stay with you until I check things out."

She nodded and closed the door so that Makita wouldn't be tempted to follow his master.

She would never be without her gun again, Evelyn promised herself, would never leave herself so vulnerable, even if she was going to miss her plane or be gone for only a few days.

As she crouched in the middle of the living room and held Makita against her, she could see the shifting beam of Amarok's flashlight through various windows as he moved around the house.

He knocked when he got back to the front. "You're right. It looks like someone cut your phone line, but I can't tell if they were also trying to peep in the windows. You have a cement pad that doesn't show any footprints since there's no mud or snow at the moment." With a scowl, he rested his hands on his hips and faced the more populated end of the street. "Whoever did it doesn't seem to be around now, though. Nothing else was disturbed. But why don't I leave Makita with you and drive around a bit, see if I can find anyone lurking in the shadows?"

She thought of the graffiti scrawled all over the inside of Hanover House, telling her to stay out of town, to go back to where she was wanted, to shut her "bleeping" big mouth, and felt foolish for getting so frightened. She'd let some disgruntled native who was leery of having a prison like Hanover House in the area reduce her to panic. "I doubt you'll find anyone," she said. "Whoever it was already did what they wanted to do—they scared me without even having to confront me."

He frowned at her. "The two boys I believe vandalized Hanover House are troublemakers. I could see them thinking a prank like this would be laughable. I'll talk to them tomorrow, see what I can find out. Until then, let me do some more searching. You can keep Makita here with you."

He was gone much longer this time. Evelyn curled up on the couch with his dog while she waited, but soon she couldn't keep her eyes open. The after-effects of the adrenaline were hitting her hard. Now that she felt safe, exhaustion soon overwhelmed her.

✦   ✦   ✦

HE'D GO BACK later, Jasper thought. He'd wait until that cocky young trooper left, then he'd punish Evelyn for ever getting involved with the bastard in the first place.

Was she sleeping with him?

The thought of her in bed with *that* man in particular, the man who'd looked at him with such a blatant challenge in his eyes at the diner, enraged Jasper. Sergeant Amarok, or whatever he'd been called, had no respect. And Evelyn was *such* a liar. She'd been on TV, telling everyone how terrible it'd been to be a victim, and how the past had cost her the ability to have a real relationship. But if she had young men showing up at her house in the middle of a Sunday night, she couldn't be struggling too badly. He'd watched her step right into the arms of that cop!

Jasper had imagined himself as being the only one to have ever been inside Evelyn, and he didn't like learning that he might have company. It ruined the fantasy. She belonged to him; she always had. He'd been her first.

But, no matter what she'd done in between, he'd be her last. That much he promised himself.

Breathing hard even though it had been at least ten minutes since he'd rushed to where he'd hidden his car and returned to the motel, he continued to pace the worn carpet between the bed and the bathroom. He'd been so close to what he wanted! One minute later, and he would've been inside her house!

But he had to admit it was better that the trooper had appeared when he did. Otherwise, they both would've had a nasty surprise, and maybe he'd be in cuffs right now. Jasper didn't plan on underestimating the sergeant, either. He looked strong, and there was no question he was confident. Maybe someone in Hilltop— *that* someone—would pose a challenge.

Or maybe not. Jasper wouldn't let anyone outsmart him. He was lucky too. He was free, wasn't he? And no one had seen him. That meant he'd have another chance.

He glanced at the digital alarm clock on the nightstand. Had the trooper left Evelyn's house yet? Or was it possible he was staying over?

The thought of that drove Jasper wild, especially because tonight was supposed to be *his* night. He longed to check, to see, but he had to be careful about how many times he drove over there. Someone could get a description of his car and report that it was in the area. The less he risked being spotted, the better. So he had to wait as much as an hour or two before heading back. Then he'd take the chance. He'd park in the secluded spot he'd used before and walk up to see if the trooper's truck was still there.

"It better not be," he grumbled and started to imagine all the things he'd do to make Evelyn suffer for such a betrayal. He'd waited twenty years for this moment; he wasn't going to have some hotshot cop take his place between her legs.

Or...maybe he *shouldn't* wait until the trooper was gone. Maybe he should break in while they were sleeping. He could hold them at gunpoint, then tie up the cop and make him watch what he did to Evelyn.

The idea of that excited Jasper beyond anything he'd felt in a long time—even finding Evelyn again.

Yes, he'd make the bastard watch, Jasper decided. That would satisfy the rage pouring through him. He'd go in another hour or so. He couldn't imagine they'd stay up even that long. It was already midnight.

He set an alarm for one-thirty—as if he'd need one— and turned on the TV to distract himself. He'd never been a patient person. He wasn't easily entertained, either. Quickly growing bored with the drama he'd put on, he flipped listlessly through the rest of the channels before throwing the remote aside and calling to check his messages. He had to use the landline to access his voicemail since there was no cell service in Hilltop, but he hadn't spoken to Hillary in two days, knew she'd be upset.

Since he was already angry, he figured this was as good a time as any to hear all the bullshit she had to say.

His wife had left him several messages. Bitching, bitching always bitching. Chelsea had sprained her foot at recess. Miranda had lost her lunch money. Who the fuck cared?

He was so sure all her messages would be the same he almost didn't listen to the last one. His finger hovered over the button that would delete it, like the others, when he heard her say something that made his heart jump into his throat.

✦   ✦   ✦

AMAROK HADN'T BEEN able to find anyone around the houses near Evelyn's. He'd even driven slowly back to town, searching for vehicles that might be loitering about the area—or were carrying the Jennings boys. He didn't see Chad or Tex or anyone who seemed remotely suspicious, so he went all the way to the Jennings' house to feel the engine of the only vehicle the family owned. It was an SUV, not a car, but he figured Evelyn could've gotten that wrong. She admitted she hadn't caught a good look at her visitor or visitors.

But the engine was cold. And the house was dark.

He stood at the edge of the property, waiting to be sure no one was moving around inside, but nothing changed in fifteen minutes or more.

If it had been the Jennings boys, they'd sure managed to get themselves home and in bed fast, he thought, especially considering they had no idea he'd be coming by.

Should he knock? He wanted to see how quickly they'd answer the door. But he took pity on their poor parents and decided he could talk to them tomorrow, like he'd told Evelyn he would. *Someone* had cut her telephone line. Even if that someone had only done it for kicks, as a scare tactic, he wanted to know if the Jennings were responsible. He also wanted to make it clear that he'd consider it stalking and would act accordingly.

By the time he returned to Evelyn's house, it was after one, and he could tell when she let him in that his knock had dragged her from a deep sleep.

"Don't wake up," he said. "Just go to bed. Makita and I will be out here, on the couch. So you don't have to worry about anything."

"You don't have to stay," she mumbled, but he took her by the shoulders, turned her around and pointed her down the hall, and she didn't attempt to argue again.

"Hey, boy," he said to Makita and shooed him off the couch so he could lie down.

✦   ✦   ✦

AS JASPER RUSHED back to Anchorage, so he could catch the first flight out in the morning, his wife's words kept echoing through his head. "Andy? I don't even know if you're listening to your messages. You're probably not. I haven't heard a word from you since you left. And I don't have any other number to reach you by. But the police came to our door this morning, while I was making breakfast. They asked a lot of questions about our car, wanted to look in it. Apparently, some teenage girl claims she saw the same make and model not far from where a woman was kidnapped two weeks ago?"

Hillary had sounded frightened, tentative, which told him that she was afraid the police might have had good reason to ask about him—and that alarmed him more than anything. He needed her on his side, needed her to retain confidence in him. How she made him appear to the authorities could be the difference between being overlooked or examined more closely.

"I-I told them that you were at job interviews that day," her message had said. "But they want to talk to you anyway. They said they'd be back. I don't know when they'll be coming. I couldn't even tell them the day you'd be home."

He was returning a lot sooner than he'd planned.

He had no choice. He had to get back and reassure Hillary, so she'd stand by him and insist that he could never harm anyone. He also had to make sure that he destroyed any and all evidence left in his hideaway, in case they wound up arresting him and went searching in that area because he or his car had been spotted down there, too.

And while he was in clean-up mode, he figured he might as well do a much better job of burying the last woman he'd killed. He'd grown over-confident, had barely thrown a few shovelfuls of dirt over her body, thinking that she could wait until he returned from having his fun with Evelyn.

He had a lot to do, and he wasn't sure he'd have the time or the opportunity to do it. But he'd be an idiot not to at least try and fix what he could while he had the chance. It could mean the difference between getting off—or going to prison for the rest of his life. He had a comfortable lifestyle, someone to pay the bills and provide sex—sex that wasn't nearly as exciting as what he got elsewhere but sex all the same—and a home. He didn't want to lose all that, didn't want to have to provide it for himself. He'd tried that before, and it was a hard and boring existence.

Still, it bothered him to be driving away while Evelyn was probably moaning with pleasure beneath that young trooper.

Jasper had had such fabulous plans for them both...

But he'd catch up with her, he promised himself,

gripping the steering wheel that much more tightly. He knew where she lived in Boston, too. Maybe it would be even more satisfying to kill her there, and bring the whole thing full circle.

Chapter 13

"I SWEAR I'VE got to buy you some groceries," Amarok said as he peered into her empty fridge.

Evelyn turned from where she was standing at the stove. "You're not excited about another bowl of oatmeal?"

He quirked an eyebrow. "Do I look excited to you?"

"Not especially." But he did look good. He *always* looked good.

"Let's go out," he said.

"I don't have time. I'll miss my flight. I have to leave in an hour."

"So miss your flight. Stay here."

She paused from stirring. "Are you kidding?"

"No."

"I can't do that! I have meetings and conference calls and... myriad things on my to do list."

"Myriad," he repeated dryly.

"Yes."

"Don't you *ever* act irresponsibly? Do something simply because you want to?"

"I wouldn't get very far with my goals if I did that."

"Okay. Never. We can work on that too." He leaned

against the counter. "So when are you coming back?"

"In a few weeks."

When he didn't say anything else, she glanced over and found him watching her with a look that made her catch her breath. "What are you thinking?"

"I want to try something."

This made her a little nervous. "What?"

"I want to hear you talk dirty."

She gaped at him. "You can't be serious!"

"Why not? They're just words. Words can't hurt you. It'll be a great place to start."

"Start what?"

He smiled. "Getting to get where we both want to go."

She didn't bother denying trying to tell him she wasn't interested, because she was. And she was intrigued by his suggestion, in spite of herself. "*How* dirty?" she asked. "Give me an example."

"Ah, so you like the idea," he said, obviously pleased.

She felt a flash of embarrassment, and a bit of insecurity too. "I'm not sure I'm capable of it."

"Sure you are. It's not hard."

"So you would like me to say...what?"

The volume of his voice dropped, and his eyes took on fresh meaning. "Are you going to fuck me when I see you again?"

Her mouth went instantly dry. "Yeah, um, that's probably not something I'd ever say, but I have to admit that it would probably work for *you*. With someone else."

He slid a little closer. "There's just one problem with that."

His gaze suddenly felt like a laser that could melt bones. "What's that?"

"I'm not interested in anyone else."

She returned her attention to the oatmeal. "Amarok, you know my story."

"We're not going to discuss 'your story' today. That's in the past. We're moving forward, and in that spirit I think you could use a few lessons."

"On talking dirty."

"Yes."

She propped one hand on her hip in a challenging pose. "And *you're* going to teach me?"

"Why not?" His grin went a little crooked—not to mention a little lecherous, but endearingly so. "We can practice while you're gone," he said. "And don't tell me you'd rather see how you do with someone else first. That's bullshit."

She shook her head. "You don't know what you're getting into. I've barely kissed a man since—"

"*Barely?*" he interrupted. "Or you *haven't* kissed a man?"

"There's been one or two."

"Dates?"

"Work associates. I pretty much steer clear of dating."

"Did you *want* to kiss them?"

"Not really."

"Well, there you go. That makes a big difference, right?"

Her gaze lowered to his lips. She wanted to kiss *him*. She'd wanted to kiss him since the first day she'd seen him pacing like a caged panther in the mayor's office, angry that she'd even propose an institution like Hanover House be built anywhere near his beloved hometown.

"Do it," he murmured.

Obviously, she'd given away her thoughts. "Do what?" she asked, playing dumb in hopes of a reprieve.

He wasn't about to allow her to back off now. "Kiss me. I can tell you're tempted. I'll let you, and I won't do anything, I swear. I won't even touch you."

She studied his square jaw, the slight cleft in the middle of his chin, the razor stubble that covered that area—and his full, soft-looking lips. "I'm afraid of where it might lead," she admitted.

"I just told you. It won't lead anywhere." He gripped the counter behind him as if to show that his hands would stay there. "One kiss before you leave. That's it." He winked. "And maybe you'll like it well enough to want another when you get back."

This was an opportunity she didn't think she could refuse—and yet she hesitated, trying to summon the nerve. Was she really going to take the initiative and kiss a man—after twenty years? Especially a man as virile as Amarok?

This wasn't just his neck. And she was sober.

"Evelyn?"

"Be prepared," she said. "I'll probably be *really* bad at this."

"There's nothing to fear. I won't be grading you."

Placing her hands on his chest, she rose up on tiptoe and touched her lips to his. She could feel the sudden intensity rise up inside them both. The power of it frightened her. But there was no refusing the compulsion that prompted her to continue.

Although his mouth opened slightly, as if he was suggesting a wetter kiss, he didn't just stick his tongue down her throat like the last guy. He waited until she opened her mouth, too, and licked his bottom lip before he responded by taking a small taste of her. He did it cautiously, gently, as if he was only exploring a little—and he didn't grab hold of her, as promised. That left her free to withdraw at any moment, and having that "out" made it so much easier to continue.

Pressing her lips more firmly to his, she deepened the kiss and felt him stiffen—but in a good way. That he liked what she was doing encouraged her. He tasted like the minty toothpaste he'd just used in her bathroom, and he smelled like her soap. "Nice," she breathed and slid her hands up his arms and over his broad shoulders until she could grab fistfuls of his thick, silky hair.

She wasn't sure exactly what happened next. Her body seemed to act of its own volition, to override her brain, because soon they were kissing so hungrily her whole body tingled with the desire to be touched. She was pretty sure she even groaned, and he did too. She was having thoughts of slipping her hands up under his shirt and kissing and licking his chest.

But then she smelled the oatmeal burning and pulled away to take the pan off the burner.

"It-it's ruined," she said while trying to come to grips with the influx of hormones that'd nearly swept her away.

He didn't respond immediately. He seemed to be holding himself rigid, trying to rein in what he was feeling, too. When he did speak, he sounded shocked. "I thought you said you weren't going to be any good at that."

"So...I did okay?"

He caught her face and turned it toward him. "The fact that I can hardly breathe right now should answer that question." He lowered his voice. "Did *you* like it?"

Heat rose to her cheeks. She found it frustrating that she could be in her thirties and still feel so young and shy. Even that was embarrassing, especially because she was the type of person who always liked to be in control of herself. But she nodded, because it was true, and he responded with a huge smile.

"Good. We'll get where we want to go," he said. "Just call me tonight for your first lesson. For someone so buttoned up and proper, I have a feeling that talking dirty might not come as naturally as kissing."

When he stepped away and called Makita, she said, "You're leaving?"

"I think that's a good note to end on, don't you?"

"What about breakfast?"

"I'll grab something in town." He leaned in to give her a quick peck as if he felt like he had to steal even that simple of a kiss. "Nice job on the zero to sixty in nanoseconds, full-on openmouthed blow-my-mind kiss, by the way. Your skills in that area won't require any work at all."

✦ ✦ ✦

THE NEXT TWO weeks were probably the happiest of Evelyn's life. Although she canceled her trip to Pennsylvania and stayed in Boston—Tim said he'd take care of that interview—she continued to work. She was too disciplined not to. But she had Amarok on her mind almost all the time, and she loved the long conversations they had on the phone at night. By the end of those two weeks they were talking even more than at night. He'd call her over lunch to say hello or to see how her day was going. Or she'd call him whenever she had a break in her schedule, just because she couldn't wait to hear his voice.

She'd never thought she'd be looking forward to moving to Alaska for any reason other than to dig in to the studies she had planned. But it now held a different kind of attraction, one that had her humming to herself for no particular reason, or staring off into space, smiling vacantly while reliving that kiss in the kitchen of her bungalow. Although she was frightened that she was finally starting a relationship, Amarok made it all seem safe, doable.

But...maybe that was because he was so far away. Sometimes she wondered how they were going to fare, given her phobias and history, once she didn't have a 3400-mile buffer.

"You're learning," he'd told her last night, in a husky voice, after she'd described, in great detail, everything she wanted to do to him.

"I'm growing bold since I don't really have to act on my words," she'd admitted with a laugh.

"The thought's there," he'd said. "That's where it all starts."

He was right. The thought *was* there. She could think of little else.

"Focus!" she told herself, as, once again, she tried to draw her mind back to what she was doing. She'd been packing up her office all day and still had a lot to accomplish before leaving Boston. She even had several things on her list that didn't include Hanover House business or preparing for the big move. Tonight, for instance, she had a cocktail party for Dr. Fitzpatrick—or Tim, as she was starting to call him. She wasn't really interested in attending it. She didn't like the attention she received in those types of social situations. But he'd invited her personally, and since he was closing down his practice to relocate to Alaska and help make

Hanover House a success, she felt as if supporting his birthday party was the least she could do.

She checked the time on her phone. Eight o'clock. Darn, she should've left already.

With a sigh, she tucked her hair behind her ears and surveyed what she had yet to pack. She had to sort through her desk and box up the contents, but she didn't have to be out for another few days. The lease didn't expire until the 31st.

Even with her busy schedule, she'd make it, she told herself, and hurried to the bathroom to repair her appearance for the party, which turned out to be far less crowded than she'd expected. It was only her, Tim and two colleagues she'd met at various forensic conferences, which made her especially glad she hadn't bailed out. They talked about Hanover House, the list of psychopaths they were having shipped there, a few new and particularly gruesome crimes that were as yet unsolved and the type of person who'd probably committed those crimes. Then they talked about Jasper and where she thought he might be living these days. That he'd never been caught seemed to come up in whatever group she was with.

Evelyn would've left after an hour, once she'd put in an appearance. But with such a small crowd, she knew it would reveal her lack of true interest. There was no melding into the background and slipping out in a gathering of four. So she stayed for several hours despite the fact that she was dying to get home and call

Amarok.

Even after holding out for so long, when she left, Tim seemed disappointed. "We were just getting started!" he complained.

"I'm moving to Hanover House before you, and have so much yet to do. I'm sorry. I've really got to get some sleep."

He put his hand over hers in what she hoped was merely a "caring" gesture. "Then...should we call you a cab?"

"No. I've only had a little wine."

He'd had much more, which was evident in the way he squinted at her glass. "*Really*?"

"It's mostly been soda water for me," she said with a laugh.

After she told everyone goodbye, she rushed to her car. Finally, she was free.

As she got in and buckled up, she listened to the voicemails Amarok had left. "God, you're all I can think about. Call me," was message number one. "I can't wait to see you again," was message number two. And "Damn! Are you ever going to call me back?" was message number three.

She chuckled to herself as she pulled out of the lot and used Bluetooth to call him back.

"*There* you are," he teased as if she'd been missing for days. "Where are you?"

"Driving from Arlington to Chestnut Hill." She told him about the cocktail party and that she'd almost finished packing up her office. And he told her that the parents of two young men—Chad and Tex Jennings—had come forward to turn in their sons for vandalizing Hanover House.

"So we know who did it?"

"I suspected them before, which is why I spoke to them and their parents."

"What kind of punishment can they expect?" she asked.

"Restitution. Probably a fine on top of that. Maybe even a few days in jail."

"Are they also the ones who cut my phone line my last night in Hilltop?"

"They claim they didn't, but maybe they're too scared to confess. They know they're already in a shitload of trouble."

"It had to be them," she said. "There's no other explanation for it."

"I think so too."

"Did they say why they did it?"

"They were just out acting stupid, which is sad, because their parents need the income they earn."

"Is this their first offense?"

"They've done other petty stuff—taking a neighbor's gnome from the yard and putting it up on the roof, skinny-dipping in hot tubs they don't own, throwing parties that get a bit too loud when their parents have been in Anchorage for medical treatment. This is by far the most serious. Most of the time, I actually like them."

"If it would help to have me talk to the judge at sentencing, I will."

"We'll see how it goes. Maybe they deserve a good scare. Maybe it'll make them take life a little more seriously."

"I just feel bad for their parents."

"So do I. But I'm merely the enforcer. I don't make the laws or have any input on the punishment."

She adjusted the heater. "Being a cop must suck sometimes."

"No more than being a psychiatrist. You must hear some terrible things."

"I do."

"How do you handle all the negativity?"

"I look for answers in it—ways to improve our penal system. Someone has to—"

"Just a sec," he broke in and covered the phone. When he came back on he said, "Can I call you back? I've got some hunters here who have questions."

"Of course," she said and got off I-95 at the Yankee Division Highway. She was almost home, couldn't wait to get inside and go to bed—and maybe visit with Amarok a bit more before falling asleep. She didn't mind losing another thirty minutes if it meant she could talk to him.

But she never made it home. Just as she came to a full stop at the traffic light a few blocks from her condo, a car slammed into her from behind.

Chapter 14

HE'D CHOSEN THE perfect time. It was late enough that the roads were deserted. But he may have hit her too hard.

Jasper waited to see if Evelyn would get out of her BMW and come to collect his insurance information and driver's license number. What he'd done couldn't be classified as a major crash, but he'd jolted her pretty good and rumpled both fenders. She should get out to at least view the damage—and when she did, he'd have her. It was too dark for her to see into his car, too dark for her to be able to ascertain that he was wearing a mask. He'd just keep his head down until she got close, as if he was hurt, and then he'd grab her. Even if she screamed, it should be okay because it would take only a couple of seconds to drag her into the car. They'd be gone before anyone could react.

But she *didn't* get out of the car. She remained inside even after the light turned green, as if she was shocked and uncertain—or maybe hurt...

"Come on, damn it," he muttered, but he realized in that moment that he'd underestimated her, after all. She was too smart to allow herself to be so easily fooled, too smart to make herself vulnerable despite normal protocol. She certainly wasn't going to risk getting hurt over a little car damage. Maybe she'd even heard of this type of trick. Since she worked in the criminal justice world, she'd probably heard everything.

Anyway, she didn't get out; she punched the gas pedal and tore around the corner.

Jasper had only a split second to decide what to do. Did he let her go *again*? Or did he chase her down?

Afraid he may never have another chance, he stomped on the gas pedal and flew around the corner, too. She wasn't going to get away from him this time, he decided. He'd smash her whole damn car, kill her that way, if he had to. How dare her think that she could stand up to him? That she could get away no matter what she did?

He thought he would wind up killing her when he raced up to the side and swerved into her. He didn't have time to mess around. He had to bring this little car chase to an end right away.

He could see the terror in her eyes, could see her mouth open in a scream—right before he forced her car into the curb. It probably would only have stopped her, if she hadn't been going so fast. Instead, it turned her car over.

Was she dead? Maybe. But he wasn't about to leave her there, wasn't about to risk that she might still be alive.

Slamming on his brakes, he skidded to a stop,

shoved the transmission into park and rushed over before the noise he'd caused could drag the people in this quiet neighborhood from the depths of sleep. She was dangling upside down, but she wasn't dead. She wasn't even unconscious. She was moaning and grabbing her seat belt as if she wanted to get it off.

"Don't worry, I've got you," he said and cut the strap before pulling her out through the broken window.

"My phone," she mumbled. "The police."

The glass had cut her in several places. He could see blood rolling down her arms. But she seemed too disoriented to fully comprehend what was going on, which was fortunate. She only knew she was afraid.

"I'll call them for you," he said and dragged her over to his car, at which point he threw her in the trunk and took off.

✦   ✦   ✦

As soon as he got a few blocks from where he'd left Evelyn's car, Jasper slowed down and removed his mask. His desire to get away from the crash site as soon as possible had to be tempered by the threat of drawing attention for driving like a bat out of hell. It was important to act as if he was just an every day guy, someone with nothing to hide. He'd found if could sell that well, most people would believe whatever story he told or whatever image he portrayed, and acting bold and confident contributed to his success.

So he calmed down and pretended as if he hadn't just kidnapped the psychiatrist so many people would recognize from TV.

He hoped he'd escaped without anyone spotting his car. It seemed like it. No one had come running. But even if he had gotten away cleanly, there was the issue of his banged up vehicle. It was obvious that it had been in an accident. As soon as possible, he needed to get off the road and stay off the road.

Which he planned to do as soon as he reached Waltham. That would take fifteen minutes. It'd be another five or ten before he could get to his hideaway.

Jasper didn't want to stop before he reached his safe spot, so he wasn't pleased when Evelyn started to scream and kick at the trunk lid. He'd disabled the release the manufacturer had installed, so she couldn't get out, but she could certainly draw attention, which meant he had to do something.

After pulling into an alley, he opened the trunk and covered her mouth with a rag dosed in a homemade version of chloroform.

"That should do the trick," he muttered when she went limp, and hopped back behind the wheel.

+ + +

AS SOON AS Amarok got home for the night, he tried calling Evelyn. It'd been only thirty minutes since he'd talked to her before, but he couldn't reach her. "Hey, it's me again," he said as he turned on the TV and lay down on the couch. "You've probably gone to bed. You could use the sleep. Good luck finishing the move out of your office tomorrow. Wish I was there to haul things around for you."

When he hung up, he didn't expect to hear from her until morning. So he was surprised to receive a call from her number only seconds later. "There you are," he said, and silenced his TV with the remote.

The person who responded wasn't Evelyn; it wasn't even a woman. "*Who is this?*"

"Who is *this*?" Amarok responded.

"Officer Pierce Schwartz, of the Arlington Police Department."

Amarok sat up. "Police department! Why do you have Evelyn's phone?"

"Can I get your name, please?"

"Of course. It's Sergeant Benjamin Murphy. I'm an Alaskan State Trooper living in Hilltop. I'm also a friend of Evelyn Talbot's. What's going on?"

"I'm afraid she's been in an accident," came the response.

Amarok's stomach twisted into knots. "Where? How? *Is she okay?*"

"We don't know," he said. "She's gone."

✦   ✦   ✦

ONCE HE PULLED deep into the copse of trees to make sure his car would remain hidden even if someone came out to this remote area, Jasper left Evelyn in the trunk and trudged down the hill to get the wagon he used to transport supplies. It was dark and there was no one around—he'd never seen anyone here—so he was breathing easier now that he was off the beaten path. But he was growing worried about the fact that she hadn't woken up yet. Had he used too much chloroform?

Those chemicals could be dangerous. And he'd been acting so fast. It wasn't as if he'd had the opportunity to measure...

As soon as he got her into the wagon, which wasn't easy since it'd been created for children and her limp body sprawled all over, he checked for a pulse—and breathed a sigh of relief when he found one. Good. Her heart was beating. That was fortunate.

Using a flashlight to avoid the briers and bigger rocks, he carted her down the hill and dumped her on the bed inside the shack.

"Welcome home," he said. "I think you're going to like what I've done to the place. For one, I haven't set it on fire yet, so that'll be an improvement." He'd been tempted. That visit Hillary had received from the police had sent him into a full-blown panic. But he was glad now that he'd held off and hadn't gone too far. Since he'd been home he'd kept a close eye on the news. He'd also spoken to the detectives who'd come by, and they didn't seem particularly suspicious of him. They were checking every car within a twenty mile radius of the kidnapping that had the same make and model as what the witness had seen and, fortunately, a lot of people in the Boston area had blue Toyota Camrys.

"Can you believe we're back together? After so long?" he said to Evelyn's inert form. "It's unbelievable, isn't it? We haven't seen each other since high school."

He took out the picture he kept in the secret compartment of his wallet and taped it to a chair, which he put in front of the bed. He wanted that to be the first thing she saw when she woke up, wanted her to know he'd be coming back for her. Then he set about tying her to the iron frame like he had the last woman. He didn't think she'd mind the old, crusty pools of blood. It wasn't easy to get a mattress down here.

"I guess I can't ask if that's too tight around your wrists," he said. Then he laughed, since he didn't give a shit anyway. He hoped it *was* good and tight, hoped it cut off the blood and made her miserable. It'd give her a taste of what she had to look forward to.

He was almost done when his cell phone rang. His wife had flown off to meet her sister in New York City so they could see a Broadway musical and spend the night at a hotel in the theater district. So what the hell was she doing calling him in the middle of the night?

He hesitated, wondering if he should answer it. If he were asleep, he wouldn't answer it. So he let it go to voicemail. Then he checked to see if she'd left a message.

"What the hell's going on?" she cried. "Chelsea just called me crying. She said she's sick. That she's throwing up, and you aren't anywhere to be found."

"Son of a bitch," he muttered and hurried up the hill to where he'd left the car so that he could get a better signal before calling her back. He'd given the girls some cough medicine that was supposed to help them sleep. He'd expected them to be knocked out until morning. So what was Chelsea doing up? He couldn't have given her too much. He'd been careful about the dosage. But maybe she was allergic to it.

Hillary answered on the first ring. "Andy? Where are you?" she asked. "You told me you'd watch the kids so that I could have this little trip with my sister!"

"I *am* watching the kids," he said. "I just ran to the store to get some Pepto Bismal. I've been sick, too. Haven't been able to keep anything down."

"Why didn't you call me?"

He stared up at the clouds moving over the moon. "Because I didn't want to bother you, didn't want to ruin your trip. And what can you do about it?"

"*So you left the kids alone?*"

"For like fifteen minutes! They were both sleeping soundly. I checked on them before I left. And I knew I wouldn't be gone long."

"You realize child protective services could take them away from us if we were to get reported, don't you? Miranda's eight and Chelsea's only six! What if you were to get in a car accident? What if you couldn't get back to them?"

"Stop freaking out!" he snapped. "I'll be with them

in a minute. Don't you even give a shit that I've been puking my guts out?"

There was a long pause. "I do. I'm sorry. I just...I was so scared there for a minute. I couldn't imagine what you could be doing this late at night."

He thought of the car and the fact that he was going to have to tell her he'd been in an accident. That wouldn't fly now. He'd have to leave the car right where it was, walk a few miles to reach a more populated area and call a cab. It'd be better, for everyone's sake, if he woke up in the morning and pretended it'd been stolen after he returned from the store. He couldn't risk having anyone notice that the paint scratches matched those on Evelyn's car, anyway, not after the police had already been around once to ask about his vehicle.

"Don't worry about anything," he said. "I'm going to be fine, and I'm taking good care of the kids."

She sniffed but seemed to be calming down. "Okay. That's nice to hear. Will you...will you call me when you get home? The kids aren't answering now."

And once he called them and instructed them to leave the phone off the hook, under the guise that he wanted to be able to hear how they were doing, they wouldn't be able to answer later, either—not until after he could get home. "Just go to bed. I've got everything handled. We'll check in come morning."

"Okay," she said, but he knew she'd be checking back regularly. He had to get his ass home as soon as possible, and that was going to take some time, especially now that he had to stop by an all-night drugstore.

"Damn kids," he muttered after he disconnected. Someday, he was going to kill them too.

Chapter 15

THE BIRDS WERE chirping so loudly that at first Evelyn thought she was sleeping outdoors. The smell of fecund earth seemed to indicate the same thing. She was close to trees and water and... nothing else that she could determine. Was she in the country?

No matter how intently she listened, she couldn't hear any cars or people or activity. What was going on?

It wasn't until she managed to lift her heavy eyelids and look around, to see the sunlight peeking through the boards of the roof overhead, that she realized where she was. Then her heart jumped into her throat, nearly choking her, as if whatever had been stuffed into her mouth wasn't enough to contend with.

She was back in the shack! Back where she'd nearly been killed!

Automatically, her hands tried to come up, to see if she was bleeding out. Had he cut her throat? She was too numb with fear to be able to feel the pain, if it was there, but she couldn't check. Although she had her clothes on, she was tied, spread-eagle to an iron bed frame.

A whimper caused her to turn her head to see who

could be making that frightened sound.

Then she realized it was coming from *her*. Her brain was so foggy, so...sluggish—and despite the numbness that'd invaded the rest of her body, her head felt like it was about to explode. The golf ball in her mouth, held in by a gag, made it so difficult to breathe. Only if she remained calm could she get enough air by dragging it in through her nose.

What'd happened? How did she come to be here? Was the person who'd abducted her a psychopath she'd studied? Or maybe another enemy—someone who didn't agree with her approach to treatment—trying to recreate the trauma of her past?

Because as much as this place looked like the shack where she'd been tormented for three days at sixteen, it couldn't be. After he'd left her for dead, Jasper had torched it.

She thought it had to be a copycat—until she saw the picture. Then her stomach cramped and she gasped, nearly sucking the ball in her mouth down her throat.

"Oh no! God, no!" she moaned, but it didn't sound like actual words. She wasn't able to articulate.

"Help me!" came out like more of a scream. "Please!" didn't sound much different. Jasper had found her. That was who'd run her off the road last night!

No, she tried to tell herself. The driver of the blue car had to be some other man, *any* other man.

But she knew in her heart it wasn't, and that knowledge made her tremble. Soon, she was shaking so badly she could feel the bed jiggling beneath her.

Where was he? The shack was so small that, unless he was under the bed, she'd be able to see him. That meant he had to be in the regular world, living whatever life other people thought he lived—like before, when he'd go to school and baseball practice as if he didn't have her tied up in a place just like this. He wasn't someone who acted odd or reclusive. He was a chameleon who behaved however he had to behave in order to blend in, be liked, escape notice.

But he wouldn't *stay* in the regular world for long. Evelyn had no illusions about that. He was too sadistic. No doubt he was already counting the seconds, anxious to return, to inflict what pain he could—which was considerable—so that he could watch her suffer.

She'd been through this once, knew what he had in store.

Squeezing her eyes closed, she tried to hold back the tears that welled up. She couldn't allow her sinuses to fill, or she'd suffocate. Even more importantly, she had to subdue her fear, which was also rising, or it would drive her mad before she could even attempt to save herself.

Concentrate! She had to put whatever minutes she had left to good use. Once Jasper returned, it wouldn't take much time for him to rape her. That was where he'd start. And it would be brutal, would probably leave her so injured she wouldn't be able to escape even if he left her untied. So, as impaired as she felt by fear and the aftereffects of whatever he'd used to drug her, she was at her strongest right *now*. She had to use that strength to her advantage; it was all she had.

Breathe. That's it. In and out...

Despite this self-talk, tears rolled into her hair as she looked around. Had he left anything behind that she might be able to use to get free? Her wrists and ankles were tied so tightly, the situation felt hopeless, but she couldn't succumb to despair. She'd never make it out of this alive if she did.

Honestly, it wasn't the dying part that scared her. It was everything that would happen before.

She saw a wagon inside the sagging front door, which had a rope tying it shut. A small table took up one corner of the shack. The chair with the picture taped to it had been arranged in front of her. Jasper had gone to great pains to recreate the "hut" they'd furnished together at one time, she realized—the lover's hideaway he'd turned into her torture chamber. There was even a throw rug similar to the one she'd once pulled out of a Dumpster so that they could make "their" place a little more comfortable.

She whimpered again, unable to help it. This was unbelievable, her worst nightmare.

Keep looking. Figure out a way to help yourself!

Besides the furniture, she saw a small refrigerator, just like they used to have for soda and alcohol, even though there was no electricity, piles of rope and cord, zip ties, a lantern, a few whips—Oh God, she knew what those were for—sacks filled with she couldn't guess what, and two or three old, dirty blankets. One looked like it had blood on it already, which made her nauseous on top of everything else.

Don't get sick! If she threw up, she'd choke on her own vomit...

Doing everything possible to gain control, to swallow the revulsion that caused the sickness, she tried to pretend as if she was just home and in bed. This was nothing but a bad dream.

Except she couldn't pretend that for long. She had to face reality, had to get out. And nothing she saw would help her, even if she could get hold of it. There were no knives, no scissors.

She was just going to have to work at her bonds until they came loose, she decided. That was her only hope.

Flexing her hands to allow some of the blood back into them, she thought of Amarok and wished he'd come, even though it was impossible. She thought about the night he'd shown up when her phone line had been cut and how she'd stepped out of her house and into his arms. It'd felt so reassuring, so good. He wouldn't want her to go through this again, she told herself. He wouldn't want her to suffer. He was trying to help her heal. Just what he'd done so far had made her feel more alive than she'd felt in twenty years.

She had to keep fighting...

She yanked on the ropes that held her feet in place,

but there was little give. She tried the same with her arms. They were tight, too. But if she could get the damn gag out of her mouth, she might be able to lean over far enough to be able to use her teeth to untie one of her hands. This was an old bed, not quite a double.

She'd started by concentrating on nothing except the need to roll that gag down so she could spit out the ball in her mouth.

Pulling her chin back toward her neck as far as possible, she used her tongue to push the ball against the fabric that was holding it in. It did no good, but she kept at it, hoping to create enough flex that she'd eventually be able to shove it through the opening she was trying to create. Then she would at least be able to use her jaws.

It was a painstaking process, so painstaking that she was soon soaked with sweat. She could hear the rasp of her own breathing, felt as if she was just this side of suffocating at all times. But it was the heat of the sun, beating down on the shack outside that frightened her most. That's what told her it was no longer early, that time was slipping away...

"It's not going to work! He's going to get here before I can even get close!" a voice wailed in her head. But somehow she silenced it, drew as much breath as she could muster and kept straining against the gag.

✦   ✦   ✦

BY THE TIME Jasper got the girls off to summer camp, it

was nearly nine. Then he had to report the Camry as stolen, which took another hour of dealing with his wife and her shock, the insurance company and then the police. By the time he was finished with it all, it was almost eleven and he felt like the day was nearly wasted, especially because Hillary wouldn't be home until late this evening, so he'd have to be back by three to pick up the girls. It'd made Hillary mad enough that he'd sent Chelsea to camp despite having thrown up in the night; Hillary wouldn't hear of her spending any time at a friend's after. "They need to spend time with their father," she'd said, making sure he understood that he was supposed to stay home with them regardless of any job interviews, training or other conflict.

Having Hillary go out of town was what had made it possible for him to kidnap Evelyn, but it was also making it difficult to spend any time with her, because he had to fulfill all the responsibilities that Hillary normally handled.

"Bitch," he muttered, hating his wife *and* her girls. He needed them. He knew that. He'd have to figure out a way to pay his own rent and living expenses without them. And yet he couldn't help resenting them at times. He'd often felt the exact same about his parents when he was growing up.

But he was free for now—for the next four hours. With drive time, that'd give him only three with Evelyn, however, which wasn't as much as he wanted.

He glanced over at the sack he'd put in the passenger seat of his wife's minivan. It contained a few new toys he was eager to experiment with. One was a stun gun.

He promised himself he'd start out easy so he wouldn't lose her as fast as he'd lost the last one. He preferred to make the pleasure last.

Once he reached the turn-off, which was merely a nondescript dirt road going into a wooded area, he watched for signs, as he always did, of other people. He couldn't see why anyone else would come here. It wasn't a place that attracted hikers or joggers. It wasn't particularly scenic, either. It was just a piece of wasteland, owned by the railroad.

Fortunately, he saw no signs of trouble. He also checked to make sure that the car he'd left the night before couldn't be seen, and was satisfied that he'd hidden it well enough. He wouldn't be able to hide the one he was driving quite as completely, but he wouldn't be at the shack for long.

Releasing his seat belt, he grabbed the sack that held the stun gun, as well as the new restraints he'd bought at an S&M store, and opened his door.

✦   ✦   ✦

EVELYN HAD HEARD the car pull up. That sound, and what it signified, brought the same sweeping, sickening fear that she'd found so debilitating when she first woke up.

Jasper was back. She was out of time—too soon.

After all she'd done to escape—after getting that gag out of her mouth and freeing her hands—she was still trying to untie one foot, and she wasn't having much success. She'd torn up her wrists; they were bleeding all over. Her hands were swollen, too—so swollen she could hardly make her fingers work.

A car door slammed.

Oh God! "Come on, come on," she murmured, but the panic rising inside her made her feel like she was about to faint. And knowing Jasper would appear within seconds had stolen the hope that'd kept her going despite the difficulty and pain involved.

This is it. It's got to happen now. Now, now, now! Focusing all her mental power on untying that last knot, she blocked out the sounds she was hearing and everything else. *Pull, damn it! Pull if you want to live! Make your fingers work!*

It was almost a surprise when the knot gave and she was able to drag her leg free. She could get off the bed—but where would she go? Jasper wasn't far. She could hear the rocks his feet dislodged rolling down some sort of incline as he drew closer. If she tried to run, he'd see her.

She'd have to incapacitate him instead. Frantically searching for some sort of weapon, she got up—and immediately collapsed. She couldn't feel her feet, couldn't walk.

The sounds of his approach grew louder. But there were no weapons, nothing she'd be able to use to fend him off—just the whips, and she had no confidence in her ability to use one of those. He'd only laugh as he took it away. Then he'd turn it on her...

There was nowhere to hide, either—except maybe under the bed, which would be so obvious it wouldn't be worth her time trying to slide under there.

She was free, and yet she was still trapped. After the valiant effort she'd put into getting away, and all the pain she'd suffered pulling and straining at those ropes, she wasn't even going to have the chance to escape.

That seemed grossly unfair...

Should she stand behind the door and try to knock him off balance when he came in? Maybe then she'd be able to get around him and run—except that her legs felt like rubber. She wouldn't make it far, and the chase would only make him angrier, more violent. She knew from past experience how explosively he reacted to *any* defiance.

Then her gaze landed on the mini-fridge. It was so small, too small for most human beings. But if she could unlatch the door, as if she'd left, and shove whatever he kept in the fridge under the blankets so she could squeeze inside, he might assume she'd already escaped and panic, flee for fear she was getting the cops.

It was her only chance, she decided.

The only problem was...even if he fell for such a trick, she knew she'd be just as likely to suffocate inside that fridge as survive.

✦ ✦ ✦

JASPER'S STOMACH PLUMMETED the second he saw that the rope he used to tie the door shut was dangling loose. Who'd opened it since he left last night? Had someone stumbled across this place and found Evelyn?

"No!" With his heart beating out a rapid tattoo, he threw the door open and stared at the bed. Sure enough, Evelyn was gone. But it didn't look like she'd been found; the fresh blood smeared all over the mattress made it look like she'd *escaped*.

"Son of a bitch!" he cried and upended the bed, threw the chair against the wall and tossed the table to the other side of the room. This was Hillary's fault, damn it! If she wasn't such a demanding bitch, always so concerned with her bratty children, he could've come earlier—and then maybe this wouldn't have happened.

How long had it been since Evelyn freed herself?

He had no idea. She could've woken up as soon as he left.

But it couldn't have been easy. The fresh blood attested to that. It also attested to how determined she was, that she insisted on fighting him.

Damn her! Where was she?

He ran outside and covered his eyes to block out the glare of the sun as he scanned the area. He didn't see anything. But even if she was close, she could be hiding in some trees or be snuggled down behind a berm. He called out for her, but it wasn't as if she'd answer him.

Even if he spent all day searching, he might not find her.

And what if she'd made it to the road already? Been picked up?

Surely, if the police weren't on their way, they'd be coming soon.

"Shit!" In a final, last-ditch effort to see if he could recover her, he checked the ground for drops of blood, hoping that might give him some indication of where she'd gone and how far she'd gotten. But he couldn't see any blood—or footprints. With all the vegetation, that'd be unlikely, anyway.

There was no other option—he had to destroy the shack and get out of there.

After hurrying up the hill to his wife's minivan, he grabbed the gas can he kept in the back and returned to his hideaway to pour it all over the mattress. Then he tossed a match on that mattress and, before he left, torched the Camry too.

Chapter 16

EVELYN COULDN'T BELIEVE Jasper hadn't seen that the door to the fridge was ajar. When he'd gone outside, she'd had to open it to gulp for air—or she'd pass out—and he'd surprised her by returning. Then she hadn't been able to get it shut all the way. But he'd been so intent on what he was doing, she didn't think he'd noticed.

She would've been glad about that, relieved—if she hadn't smelled gasoline.

The shack was a tinderbox to begin with, and he'd just added an accelerant. If she didn't get out fast, she'd burn to death. But the loud crackle made it difficult to know where he was, since she could no longer hear him. Was he outside watching the place burn? Could he be hoping to flush her out?

Paranoia tempted her to think that way, to believe that he knew more than he probably did. The frightened child inside her tried to convince her to remain hidden, because that fridge, especially now that it was encircled by fire, seemed like the only place he couldn't reach her. She was afraid if she scrambled out and headed for safety, she'd only run into him, and she had no illusion that it would be any better fate than dying where she was.

But then she thought of Amarok, and her parents and sister, and her work. She'd told herself for years that she wouldn't allow Jasper to get the best of her. She'd fought that first experience with everything she had. Why would she let him win in the end?

She wouldn't, she decided. She was going to survive. Again. And then she'd do everything in her power to see that he was finally punished so he could no longer hurt her or anyone else.

The heat was already unbearable, and smoke hung so thick in the air, she couldn't breathe. Coughing and gasping, she pushed herself out of the fridge and onto the dirt floor. She could see flames licking their way up to the roof, knew the whole shack could crumble on top of her any second. Yet she could hardly move, still didn't have complete control of her body. Curling up inside that fridge had done nothing to get the blood flowing back into her limbs, so she was as numb and tingly as she'd been before—not to mention weak, hungry and exhausted.

Move! Now! she ordered herself. The fire was consuming the shack like a piece of paper. If she waited any longer, she'd burn right along with it.

Remaining low to the ground, she dragged herself to the entrance. The flames had caught hold of the door, but she grabbed that old, bloody blanket she'd spotted earlier and used it to protect her from the flames as she crawled across the threshold.

Part of her believed Jasper would grab her immediately. But once she reached the cool embankment of a creek and rolled over onto her back to stare at the sky overhead, she realized she was alone.

She stayed there, gulping for breath until she also realized something else—if she didn't get up, he'd escape. She had to get a good look at him, note the license plate number on his car, something. Otherwise, she could spend the rest of her life as she'd spent the past twenty years, wondering if he was around the very next corner.

Driven by sheer determination, Evelyn staggered to her feet. But she'd been unconscious when he brought her here, had no idea where she was, or, now that she was no longer in the shack, from which direction she'd heard his car approach. Fear, panic and desperation had a tendency to distort perceptions, which was also a problem.

By the time she saw the smoke of a second fire, and could walk well enough to climb the embankment to reach it, she was fairly certain he was gone—and so were the license plates on the burning vehicle he'd used to abduct her.

✦   ✦   ✦

THE MAN AND woman who picked Evelyn up on the side of the road wanted to take her to the hospital, but she'd demanded they drive straight to the closest police station. She had some superficial wounds—bloody chafing on her wrists and ankles, cuts on her arms and the sides of her mouth and some burns on her legs (even though she hadn't been aware of ever coming into direct contact with the fire). But it was probably her headache that bothered her most. She needed to be treated at some point, if only to have the stitches from Hugo's attack removed and to make sure that whatever Jasper had put on that rag hadn't caused permanent damage.

But she didn't dare waste any time. She wanted to tell the police everything she knew, get them out searching the area where she'd been found before the evidence Jasper was trying to destroy could be destroyed—if it wasn't too late already. That was also why she'd used the man's cell phone to call 9-1-1 the instant she got the couple who'd helped her to pull over.

"You really shouldn't be sitting here. We can talk in the hospital." This came from a young, clean-cut detective by the name of Mike Hampton. Evelyn was sitting in his office with a blanket draped around her shoulders and a cup of coffee waiting on the ledge of his desk.

"Admittance takes forever," she said. "We need to act now."

"We are acting now," he assured her. "I've got a team out there, but they can't do anything with that building he burned, or the car, until it all cools off."

She pressed her fingers to her temples. "How long

will that be?"

"A few hours, maybe more."

"And then it'll be dark," she muttered, irritated by the limitations that hampered police progress while Jasper seemed able to get away with whatever he pleased.

Detective Hampton ignored her sarcasm. "Meanwhile, why don't I take your statement, write down everything you recall while its fresh in your mind?"

Evelyn was eager to go over it all. She told him what she'd told the sergeant at the front desk when she first hurried into the police station, only in greater detail. But as she spoke, she realized that she didn't have a lot to offer as far as the kind of details that might differentiate Jasper from any other man.

"So you didn't get a look at his face," the detective said.

She hugged the blanket closer. "No. He-he was wearing a ski mask."

"When he came this morning, too?"

"I can't say. I was crammed into the refrigerator by the time he entered the shack."

Hampton checked his notes. "You said the door to the refrigerator was open when he came back, that you were shocked he didn't notice."

"That's true, but...I couldn't see him, couldn't see anything. My head was curled into my knees. I'd used my elbow to crack the door to give me a little ventilation, which is why I couldn't pull it closed fast enough."

"And you're sure the car he burned is the car he used to abduct you?"

"It had to be. It was a blue sedan that ran me off the road. I was in too much of a panic to get his license plate number when he was coming after me. I was just trying to get away, to survive. But this morning I looked for license plates, and...he'd taken them off."

"Then I'm guessing he filed the VIN number off, too," he said with a frown. "But...we'll look for that, of course, when we can."

She nodded.

"What makes you so sure the man who nearly killed you twenty years ago is behind this latest attack?" he asked. "Did he say something specific, or...?"

She craved the bolstering effects of the coffee he'd provided, but her hands weren't steady enough to bring the cup to her lips, so she continued to let it grow cold. "No. We-we didn't have a chance to interact. It was that picture he left taped to the chair that told me."

"Your prom picture."

"Yes. Who else would have access to that?"

He didn't bother to answer that question. "What about a description?" he asked. "I understand you didn't see his face. But can you tell me anything about his general size and body shape?"

"He was tall, strong—pulled me out of my over-turned car as if I weighed nothing."

"Can you guess at his height?"

She hesitated. "I can only give you those details for

when I knew him in high school." Damn it! Nothing else was clear enough.

"And he could've grown since then. Some boys do." The detective bent his head as he read over his notes. "Well, we'll see what we can find at the scene. Maybe we'll get lucky and come up with a shred of evidence that will give us an indication as to where he's living."

"Thanks," she said and tried to remain hopeful. But later that day, when they could actually start looking, they admitted that everything had been destroyed. The only thing they found was a shallow grave not far from where the shack had been.

It contained the body of a woman who'd been abducted three weeks earlier.

✦ ✦ ✦

BY THE TIME Hillary got home, Jasper had half the house packed.

"What's going on?" she asked, obviously shocked.

The kids were asleep, so he kept his voice down. "We're moving."

She dropped her purse. "*Why?*"

"Because you never wanted to come here to begin with."

"But...what about my job?"

"You're a nurse. You can get a job anywhere, especially with your references. You don't like the hospital you're at right now, anyway, remember? You've told me as much."

"I didn't say I couldn't make do, get used to it."

"You shouldn't have to."

She came deeper into the room. "There are other considerations, Andy. What about the lease on this house?"

"What about it? It's month-to-month. We'll give our landlord a check for September and be out of it."

"That'll cost us an extra thousand bucks!"

"Won't it be worth a thousand bucks to be able to live in Arizona, like you wanted to begin with?"

She thought about that for a moment. "I-I guess," she said at length. "But...what about the Camry? Will we leave without it?"

"Of course. Either the cops will find it, or the insurance will replace it. That's no reason to stay."

"It's just...this is so sudden. And we haven't been here very long."

He taped another box closed. "I know. It was a mistake to come. I really thought I'd get that job, that I'd be able to make our lives better. Then I didn't, and you've been so disappointed that I haven't been able to find something else. Maybe we'll have better luck in Phoenix. At least we'll have a mild winter, right?" He grinned at her. "I want to give you what *you* want for a change. You deserve it. Think about it...if we bail now, it won't affect the kids half as much as if we wait. It'll just be like we had a...a six-week vacation in Boston one summer."

Her eyes filled with tears. "So we can really go

where I want to go? By my family?"

"Of course. Since you've been gone, I've realized how much you do every day. I don't support you enough, Hill. I need to pitch in more, make sure you're happy. And getting you out of here is the first step."

She dashed a hand across her cheeks. "So you still love me."

The disbelief in her voice prompted him to put his arms around her. He *didn't* love her—sometimes he even wondered what love was—but he knew she'd expect such physical comfort. "Of course I do. You're the best thing that's ever happened to me."

"You've been so remote lately. So...moody and...and angry. I didn't know what you were thinking. I assumed...I assumed you were tired of me, or bored, or—"

"I've just been depressed," he said. "Who wouldn't be? I haven't been able to get a job. That makes me feel worthless. But I'll find something in Arizona. I'm going to make you proud. I promise."

Her arms slid around his neck, and she buried her face in his shoulder.

It irritated him how gullible she was. If he really cared about her, she wouldn't have to wonder. That seemed obvious to him. But she was reacting exactly as he'd hoped, so he played into it, as if he felt far more than he really did. "Are you okay?"

She sniffed. "I'm fine. Just...happy that everything's still good between us, I guess. And that I'll soon be living close to my mom and sister."

"Every couple has their hard times," he said. "But that doesn't mean there isn't something that draws us inexplicably together." Take him and Evelyn, for example. She infuriated him, so much that he was tempted to go after her again right away. But he knew that wouldn't be wise; she'd be ready for him this time. So he'd sit back for a year or two, until she began to feel comfortable again. Maybe she didn't realize it, but he knew where she was going. He even knew the specific house where she would soon live. So he'd keep an eye on the news, follow developments in her career and what went on at Hanover House. Then, when the time was right, he'd pay her another visit.

And this time, she wouldn't get away.

"*Inexplicably*?" Hillary echoed. The confusion on her face told him he'd used the wrong word, a word she didn't find as reassuring as she would've liked.

"Undeniably," he corrected. "I couldn't live without you." At least not for free. "We're going to make it," he promised and gestured at all the boxes. "So are you in? Should we get out of here?"

"As soon as we can," she replied.

He smiled. "I don't see any reason we can't drive off by tomorrow night."

✦   ✦   ✦

SINCE SHE'D BEEN abducted the night before, Amarok had stayed in close contact with the police. They told Evelyn he'd been so worried that he'd booked a flight to

Boston so he could look for her himself. It was only that he'd heard word she'd been found that stopped him.

She was glad he'd decided to stay. She'd be returning to Alaska soon enough; it wasn't necessary for him to leave Hilltop. That he'd even considered coming to Boston surprised her. This city would be so foreign to him. And they hadn't been friends for long enough to warrant such an expense.

But she knew he was worried about her. So, after letting her parents know she was safe, she called Amarok.

"They're not going to catch him," she said into the phone, after explaining exactly what'd happened and assuring him that she was just fine.

"He's smart," Amarok said. "Bold, too."

"He's been out there killing for twenty years. As far as I'm concerned, the body they found proves it. Surely, that's not the only one. He's still active, and he'll remain active until someone stops him."

"It must be hard to know that."

She pulled the blankets higher. "It is. It was easier to think he'd mysteriously disappeared—or killed himself, as his parents suggested."

"The police will catch him someday, Evelyn."

She knew he was just trying to comfort her. It was very possible they'd never catch him. He was too damn smart, too damn good at killing. "I can't believe I got away. When I look back... It was a miracle," she said, unable to explain how she hadn't ended up in a shallow grave like that other woman.

"How'd he find you in the first place?" Amarok asked. "That's what I want to know."

"He must've been following me."

"But he couldn't have run across you randomly."

"Oh, you mean to begin with. I have no idea. But if he's back in Boston, why haven't the police been able to find *him*?"

"There are a lot of people in Boston, and it's been a long time. I'm guessing he looks different. That can't sound like much of an excuse to you, but...it's not easy to catch a lust killer, and if anyone can say why, it'd be you."

"I know. I just can't believe I'm going to have to continue to live with the thought that he's out there, somewhere." She thought of all the other victims in the world, who never achieved resolution, and felt guilty for complaining. Why should she be any different? And what about those who'd lost their lives? At least she'd survived and escaped. She should be grateful, not allow her bitterness to overtake her gratitude. "But I'm not the only one dealing with this type of thing," she added. "I realize that. I'll cope with it, somehow."

"I don't want you going back to your condo, not even to get your stuff," he said. "Send half a dozen brawny men to get it for you, and be done with that place."

"Agreed. I won't go back. Tomorrow, when I get out of the hospital, I'm going to rent a room from someone in Cambridge. My parents want me to stay with them, but I can't. I have to find a random place, a place where I know Jasper would have *no* way of finding me."

"Or you could move here right away, instead of waiting." He said that like he wanted to see her, to watch over her.

"This couldn't happen in Hilltop, could it, Amarok?" she asked, suddenly uncertain that she'd be safe *anywhere*. "That night when my phone line was cut—"

"I'm hoping that was just scare tactics," he broke in. "Like we talked about. It's the best explanation we've got, at any rate."

She stared up at the ceiling. "So you think I'll be safe there."

"I want to say you will. I'll do everything in my power to look out for you. But the truth is, that kind of shit could happen anywhere. It all depends on how determined Jasper is, right?"

"At least I'll be 3400 miles away from Boston. So many bad things have happened to me in this city. I'm ready to leave. Now even my mother wants me to get out."

"Whoa, Lara's finally supportive of Alaska?"

She allowed her eyes to close. "I wouldn't say she's *supportive*. At this point, Alaska's just the lesser of two evils. What she'd really like is for me to get a safer job, stay out of the media and disappear into another city, like Los Angeles or Seattle."

"I thought she didn't want you so far away?"

"She claims they'll move with me."

"And your sister?"

She covered a yawn. "She'd probably stay. She likes Boston. She's got a great job running a major hospital, so she makes good money, and she loves her work."

"You and your sister are definitely high achievers. So...are you tempted by what your mother suggests?"

"I was for a second," she admitted. "It just sounds so...safe."

"You'd give up Hanover House?"

She snuggled lower in the bed. "No. You're right—I couldn't. It's hard to explain, but...I have to do what I'm doing even if my folks don't like it." She gripped the phone tighter. "Even if *you* don't like it. Because nothing's really changed. I won't let Jasper or anyone else drive me into a corner. Not when I can use the knowledge I've gained, and what I might learn in the future, to fight back, to make a difference."

"It's what's bringing you here, so I'm not complaining," he said.

She smiled at his response. "Would you like to know how I hung on mentally? How I got through it?"

"Of course."

She rolled onto her side and spoke more softly. "By thinking of you. I wanted to live so that I could see you again."

"I like that," he said. "But if that's the case, why can't I talk you into coming tomorrow?"

She laughed. "Because I have too much to do here!

I'll come as soon as I can." There was a noise at the door as her parents and sister rushed in, carrying flowers and balloons and candy.

"Evelyn!" her mother cried.

"Amarok, my family's here," she said into the phone. "And I'm exhausted—and a little groggy from the relaxers they've given me. Can I call you tomorrow?"

"Of course."

"Goodnight."

"I can't wait for you to return," he said.

Evelyn thought of those words an hour later, after her family had left. That was the last thing to go through her mind before she fell asleep, and the first thing when she woke up. As a matter of fact, she was still thinking about Amarok mid-morning, when a courier carried in a dozen long-stem red roses.

The card read: "I've never had a better kiss. Amarok."

Epilogue

TWO WEEKS LATER, Evelyn was packing her suitcase for her big move—she flew out the next morning—when her father came in with her mail. She'd had what was going to her post office box forwarded to a different post office entirely—and a box in his name—and asked him to pick it up for her, since she wouldn't go anywhere she'd ever been before.

"It looks like you'll be up late, if you plan to read through all of this," he said, dropping a big stack on the bed.

Evelyn sat down to sort through it. She needed the break.

Most were letters of support from other victims. A lot of those letters contained checks from people wanting to contribute to her research. Evelyn was always touched by the fact that so many people were willing to get behind a good cause—and was glad that at least a portion of the population understood the need for what she was doing.

But amongst all the letters and checks, bills and junk mail, she found a postcard of San Quentin State Prison and knew, even before she turned it over, that it was from Hugo Evanski.

Dear Dr. Talbot,

I was saddened to hear of your recent and very unfortunate experience with Jasper Moore. How interesting that he has surfaced after so long. You must be shocked—or maybe not. You, of all people, must understand just how determined a killer can be.

I can't help but admire his tenacity. But if I admire his tenacity, I also have to admire yours. Kudos on saving your own life. You're obviously very spirited—a worthy opponent.

I look forward to getting to know you better in Hilltop.

Yours truly—Hugo Evanski

HANOVER HOUSE is the prequel to Brenda's new suspense series, which will be released from St. Martin's Press beginning September 2016. You can join Evelyn Talbot and Sergeant Amarok as Hanover House opens its doors in Book #1, HER DARKEST NIGHTMARE. In the following excerpt, you will meet Anthony Garza, one of its chilling new psychopaths:

They'd had to sedate him. That was what the marshals told Evelyn. They'd said he was so difficult and dangerous, to himself and others, that the only way to get Anthony Garza safely from one place to another was to medicate him. A registered nurse at ADX Florence in Colorado where he'd been incarcerated before had administered 300 milligrams of Ryzolt four hours ago.

There was a note of it on his chart.

But the tranquilizer had worn off by the time he arrived at HH. According to the correctional officers in receiving he'd come in slightly agitated and, despite his chains and cuffs, had quickly grown violent, going so far as to head-butt an officer. At that point, someone had sounded the alarm while others wrestled him to the ground and replaced his cuffs with a straightjacket, further restricting his range of motion. Now he had four officers flanking him instead of two.

Although they stood with him in the holding cell across from her, even had to support him so he wouldn't trip on his ankle chains, he wouldn't settle down. He was raving like a lunatic, threatening to dismember anyone he came into contact with.

"I won't stay in this Godforsaken place!" he cried. "You'll all be fucked if you make me. Do you hear?"

"Should we take him to his cell?" It was Officer Whitcomb who asked. He obviously doubted she'd be able to get anything meaningful out of Garza when the man was in such a state, and she had to agree. She'd been about to suggest they take him away and give him a chance to cool off. But the second Mr. Garza realized she was on the other side of the glass, he fell silent and went still.

"Who are you?" His dark eyes shined with anger-induced madness as they riveted, hawklike, on her.

Prepared for an ugly encounter, should it go that way, Evelyn fixed a placid expression on her face. She couldn't, wouldn't show this man how unsettled he made her. If he thought he was the first to use intimidation, he was sadly mistaken. Even the sudden reversal in his behavior came as no surprise. Sometimes the men incarcerated at HH reminded her of actors in a play with how quickly and easily they could slip in and out of whatever character suited them best.

"Ah, you're coherent after all," she said. "So what have you been doing, Mr. Garza? Putting us on notice that you're no one to be messed with?"

He didn't answer the question. "*Who are you?*"

She put on the glasses she used to alleviate eyestrain and jotted a note on his chart. *Low frustration tolerance. Possibly disorganized thinker and yet...seems more calculating than that.*

Aggressive when fearful or uncertain or presented with unfamiliar stimuli—

"Hey! I asked you a question!" He half-dragged the C.O.s along with him so he could shuffle up to the glass.

The guards started to yank him back, to show him that he'd better not get out of control again. No doubt they were angry about before. One of their fellow officers had been shuttled off to medical nursing a broken nose because of Garza hitting him with his head. But, lowering her clipboard, Evelyn motioned for them to leave him be. She was here to study, not punish. That distinction was important to her own humanity. "I'm your new doctor."

"No, you're my next victim," he said. Then he made kissing noises and smiled, revealing the jagged, broken front teeth he'd gotten from gnawing at the cinderblock wall of his last cell.

Want me to let you know when HER DARKEST NIGHTMARE, the next story in the exciting new Evelyn Talbot Chronicles comes out? Just provide your email address, and I'll send you a note!

Sign-up for my newsletter at www.brendanovak.com

And turn the page for the first chapter of HER DARKEST NIGHTMARE, due out September 2016.

Her Darkest Nightmare

"Kill one and you might as well kill twenty-one."
—Mark Martin, British Murderer

Prologue

WHEN SHE CAME to, Evelyn Talbot could hear nothing. She couldn't see anything, either. Darkness had fallen, and the shack, where she lay on the cool dirt floor, didn't have electricity.

Or...was she no longer in the shack?

Her thoughts were fuzzy....

Maybe she was *dead*. She'd been expecting death, been thinking that, unlike most people, she wouldn't live long enough to graduate from high school. If she were alive, there would be pain. There'd been plenty of that in the three days Jasper Moore had held her captive in this place. Yet, in this moment, she felt...nothing.

That made no sense.

Unless she'd dreamed the whole thing. Was it all just a terrible nightmare? Would she wake up and go to school to find Jasper hanging out near her first period class, lounging against the wall along with some of the other guys on the baseball team, talking about where they should eat dinner before prom?

She imagined telling him that she'd dreamed he killed Marissa, Jessie and Agatha—all three of her best friends. They'd have a good laugh, blame it on the horror movie they'd seen together not long ago, and he'd sling his arm around her neck and draw her in for a kiss.

That would fix everything, put her world right.

But the brief flash of hope that shot through her didn't last. Her own bed didn't feel like the lumpy, hard-packed earth. Even the old mattress they'd dragged out here when they first found this place and made it their secret hideaway didn't feel *that* uncomfortable. As soon as she inhaled, she could smell smoke and remembered Jasper tossing a lighted match on some kindling he'd gathered from the forest. He'd sat there, on one of the stools they'd also brought to this place, for what seemed like forever, smoking a joint. He'd never smoked weed before, at least not around her, and they'd been together for six months. But *this* Jasper Moore wasn't the boy she'd known; *this* Jasper Moore was a monster.

While he studied her, she hadn't dared to so much as twitch. She'd kept her eyes closed, couldn't see what he was doing. But she'd had the feeling he was watching her carefully, waiting to be sure she was dead.

Since he'd released her from the rope he used to tie her up, she'd had the use of her hands. It had been all she could do not to use them to staunch the blood pouring from her neck. She could hardly keep from gurgling as she breathed—and the smoke that thickened the air made those shallow breaths even more difficult.

She'd thought she might suffocate if she didn't bleed to death first. But gut instinct had told her that her last and only chance depended on convincing him he'd finished the job he set out to do when he slit her throat.

"That'll teach you to mess with me, bitch," he'd muttered when, at long last, he walked out, leaving her to the fire he'd started to destroy the evidence.

Once he was gone, she'd tried to get up, but she must've blacked out. It had been light then, light enough that she'd pictured him hurrying home so he wouldn't be late for baseball practice. He'd attended school while keeping her out here. When he returned each night, he'd laugh and tell her how frantic the whole community was to find her and her friends—even what various kids and teachers were saying at school—as if he found it quite thrilling. He'd talk about the prayer circles, the yellow ribbons and the anxious news reporters that were hounding everyone she knew for the smallest detail. When she asked him how he was able to keep slipping away to come back to the shack, he'd explained that he told everyone he was going out searching, too. The worried boyfriend was a part he claimed to play well, and she had no doubt of it. He could play *any* part.

He'd certainly fooled her.

If only someone would realize he wasn't sincerely upset and take a closer look at him! But that would never happen. With his chiseled face, athletic body, sharp mind and rich parents, he was so convincing, so believable, so unlikely a killer. No one would *ever* suspect him of committing a crime like this.

Squeezing her eyes closed, she struggled to staunch the tears that welled up. That he could betray her love in such a terrible way was the worst of what she'd suffered. But she couldn't focus on the heartbreak. That would only make her situation worse. She had to concentrate on *breathing* or maybe she'd simply...stop.

The fire must've burned itself out. She had no idea why it hadn't consumed her *and* the shack, as Jasper had intended, but below that acrid scent she identified the sweet, cloying smell of decaying flesh. The stench had been getting worse, more stomach-churning every day. Jasper had said it made him hard to have her friends watch, with their sightless eyes, what he did to her. He said they were all just hanging out together, having fun like old times—except her friends had finally shut their big mouths.

What he'd done to them made her skin crawl. How he talked about it, with such relish, was almost as bad. She couldn't escape the vision she'd seen when she'd come looking for him—and surprised him while he was posing their bodies like mere mannequins. He'd said he killed them because they "tried to make her break up with him" by telling her he'd hit on Agatha at a party a week ago—as if their loyalty somehow made all of this *their* fault. He'd said he wouldn't allow *anyone* to cause trouble for him.

He'd claimed he hadn't been planning to kill *her*,

but he certainly hadn't acted as though he minded, as though she was any different or more special to him than they were. As a matter of fact, the more pain he caused her, the happier he became. The torture had ignited something in him, changed him. She'd never imagined anyone could be like that.

But she wasn't dead yet. If she could smell what she could smell and feel what she could feel, the darkness was simply that—darkness. And her muddled thoughts? Whose thoughts wouldn't be muddled after what she'd suffered? She had to fight the heaviness that dragged at her limbs and seemed to slow her heart, fight for her life. At least she didn't have the fire to contend with. Good thing she'd been on the floor, below the smoke, or she probably would've died.

If she could make it to the highway, maybe she could flag down a passing motorist.

Lifting a heavy, unwieldy hand to her throat, she felt the stickiness of her own blood. She was lying in a pool of it. But the gaping slash in her throat wasn't her only injury. She had a broken leg—it was crooked, which left little question—and had various other injuries. She could see out of only one eye and, in three days, hadn't eaten anything except the gross substances he'd forced down her throat while enjoying the humiliation he caused.

Did she have even *half* a chance?

It was too late, she decided. No one could be expected to survive what she'd endured. She should use her last moments on earth to scratch a message into the dirt so that her family would know it was Jasper who'd killed her. At least then he wouldn't get away with it.

But thought of her parents created such a tremendous longing—and empathy for how they would feel to find her so badly used and broken—that she managed, with massive effort, to sit up. When she didn't pass out again, she took heart and, feeling for something solid, grabbed Jasper's stool to help drag her to her feet.

That was when the pain started. Why it suddenly rushed upon her out of nowhere, she couldn't begin to guess. But the moment she came upright, her entire body screamed out in protest. And when she put pressure on her leg—oh God! She nearly lost consciousness.

Focus! Keep standing! Push the pain away! Think of only one thing—what to do next!

That was getting out of the place where her friends had been murdered—where he'd asked them to meet him so they could have a "private talk."

She feared Jasper would somehow realize the shack hadn't burned and come back to investigate. But if she was going to live, she had to move *now*. In five minutes, or less, she might not have the strength or the presence of mind.

Considering the agony of every footfall, Evelyn had no idea how she managed to stagger through the rain-drenched woods. She wasn't even sure she was moving in the right direction. It didn't matter that she'd traversed the small path to the shack at least a hundred times. There was greenery everywhere, and it all looked the same. She could be going in a circle, but she had to keep moving, keep struggling—had to find someone to help her.

Not until she was in the road did she realize that she'd reached her goal—and then it occurred to her only because a car horn sounded as a vehicle came at her. The blast was intended to get her out of the way, but she couldn't take another step, couldn't even raise her arms to signal her distress.

She heard the brakes squeal as the driver swerved to miss her, heard the crunch of gravel as the car came to a stop. Then she crumbled and would've died right there on the dotted yellow line separating the two lanes of pavement if not for the man who came rushing toward her, shouting, "Oh my God! What *happened* to you?"

Chapter 1

"We are all evil in some form or another."
–Richard Ramirez, the Night Stalker

Twenty years later...

HE'D KILL HER if he could. He'd attacked her once before. She had to remember that.

Dropping her pen on top of the notepad she'd carried in with her, Dr. Evelyn Talbot slipped her fingers under her glasses and rubbed her eyes. She hadn't gotten much sleep last night; she'd had another of her terrible nightmares. "The Plexiglass is there for a reason, Hugo. It will always be between us. And we both know why."

This wasn't the answer he'd been hoping for. Impatience etched lines in his moderately handsome face, with its wide forehead and innocent-looking brown eyes, but he was careful not to raise his voice. In fact, he did the opposite: he lowered it in appeal. "I won't lay a hand on you, I swear! I just have to tell you something. Come over to this side so I can whisper. It'll only take a minute."

It would take even less time for him to get his hands

around her throat, or put her in the hospital, like he did when she first met him at San Quentin.

Reclaiming her pen, she replied in the same measured tone she always reserved for her subjects. "You know I can't do that. So say what you have to say. Do it right here, right now. We've been going around and around with this for two weeks."

He twisted to look up at the camera being used to monitor his behavior. Whenever she met with an inmate, a correctional officer in a room down the hall viewed the proceedings on closed-circuit TV. The inmates thought they were being watched for security purposes, but these sessions were also recorded. The video enabled her to study the nuances in their body language, which was, in addition to their speech patterns, the focus of her research.

"I *can't*," he insisted. "Not in front of the cameras. I'm a dead man if I do."

Someone had him convinced. She believed that much. Although, with the way her subjects lied, she could easily be wrong. Maybe he was making it all up. "But *who* would harm you?" She leaned closer. "And how?"

Evelyn had been studying Hugo Evanski since Hanover House opened three months ago, in November. He'd been among the first of the psychopaths transferred here, had scored a whopping thirty-seven out of forty on The Hare Psychopathy Checklist, or PCL-R. But to look at him or talk to him, no one would know he was capable of murder. From the beginning, Evelyn had found him to be intelligent, tractable and, for the most part, polite. He was even helpful, when he could be.

The thought made her a bit uneasy, but if she had a friend among the psychopaths she'd come to Alaska to analyze, it would be Hugo. Maybe that was why she was tempted to trust him, even after what he'd done before and everything else she'd been through.

"I was right about Jimmy, wasn't I?" he said.

A month and a half ago, he'd warned her that another inmate was planning to hang himself with a sheet. If not for Hugo, Jimmy Wise would be dead.

"Yes, but you didn't demand I risk my life to get that information."

"Because Jimmy was no threat to me!"

"So who is?"

Squeezing his eyes closed, he tapped his forehead against the glass.

Evelyn waited.

"What can I do?" he asked when he spoke again. "How can I get you to believe me? To give me just a moment of privacy?"

He'd strangled fifteen women and he'd injured her. That meant there was *nothing* he could do because she wasn't stupid enough to put herself in jeopardy.

"I'm sorry," she said. "I truly am."

His gaze fell to the four-inch-long scar on her neck. "It's *his* fault."

She touched the raised flesh. She supposed, in a way, Hugo was right. But she found it amusing that he assumed no personal responsibility for his own behavior the day they met. She could've pointed that out, but was more interested in what he hoped to tell her. "Yes."

Getting up, he paced the length of the small cubicle that comprised his half of their meeting space—what constituted her "couch." "I would never let anything happen to you," he said, "not if I could help it."

"And what happened at San Quentin?" This time she couldn't resist....

"I didn't know you then. Things are different now."

Were they *really*? That was the question.

"I appreciate the sentiment," she responded, but that didn't mean she'd change her mind.

He stopped and pivoted to face her. "You don't understand. *You're not safe*. None of us are."

The intensity of his voice and expression made the hair on her arms stand on end. Is that what Hugo was hoping to do? Frighten her?

She had to admit it was working—but only because he'd never taken this tact before January 1st. And he seemed so convinced, so sincere.

Apparently, even *she* could still be taken in....

Grabbing her pad and her pen, Evelyn stood. "I'm afraid we'll have to end our session early. You're so obsessed with...whatever it is that's causing your agitation we can't make any progress."

"Wait!" He rushed the glass. "Evelyn..."

When she gaped at him for using her first name as if they were familiar enough for him to do that, he reverted to the usual formalities.

"Dr. Talbot, listen to me. Please. This prison houses psychopaths, right? Men who take lives without hesitation or remorse."

She made no reply, didn't see where one was necessary. He was stating information they both knew to be accurate.

"I'm trying to tell you that—" he glanced at the camera again "—not every killer at Hanover House is locked up."

This was the last thing she'd expected. "What are you talking about?"

"That's all I'll say. Unless...unless you can give me a chance to speak to you in private. I'll explain what I know, what I've seen and heard. And I won't hurt you. *I'm trying to help!*"

Evelyn refused to listen to any more of this. Clearly, Hugo was hoping to gain some type of control in their relationship by acting like her protector at the same time he chipped away at her peace of mind. No way would she allow him to do that. At just sixteen, her life had nearly been taken when she fell in love with a man like Hugo. After becoming a psychiatrist eight years ago, she'd devoted her life to unraveling the mysteries of the remorseless killer. She knew more about the psychopathic mind than anyone else in the world, except, maybe, Dr. Robert D. Hare, who developed the

PCL-R and had been researching the same subject for nearly thirty years. But, sadly, even she didn't know as much as she wanted, not nearly enough to protect the unsuspecting.

"We'll meet at our regular time day after tomorrow," she told him. "Do what you can to relax. You're growing paranoid."

She walked out, but he didn't let it go at that. "You'll see," he called after her. "You're going to wish you'd believed me!"

✦　✦　✦

WITH A SIGH of bone-deep exhaustion, Evelyn tossed her notepad on her desk and slid into her chair.

"What's wrong? Another headache?"

The sound of Lorraine Drummond's voice at her open door brought Evelyn's head up. "No, I just left a session with Hugo Evanski."

Lorraine, who'd answered an ad in the newspaper when Evelyn and the warden began staffing the center last September, was heavyset, in her mid-fifties and recently single. She had a small house in Anchorage an hour away, two grown children and no education beyond high school. She hadn't even worked until her divorce, but she was doing a terrific job of running the center's food service program.

"Since he came here, Hugo's been perfect. You told me that yourself."

"He's changing. Acting strange."

"Why not pass him along to Dr. Fitzpatrick or one of the others? Give yourself a break?"

"Dr. Fitzpatrick is already using him for some of his studies—and has been since we opened. I can't ask him to do more. Not since Dr. Brand quit and Dr. Wilheim came down with the shingles. We're barely managing without them. Who knows how long it'll be before we can find someone to replace Ely and Stacy's able to come back to work?" Besides, Evelyn felt duty-bound to carry the heaviest load. She was largely the reason they were all stuck in the middle of nowhere with thirty-seven of the worst serial killers in America. The other 213 inmates were also diagnosed as psychopathic but were in for lesser crimes and would one day be released.

"You could if you wanted to," Lorraine insisted.

"I don't want to. There're only five other productive members of the team right now. I can handle him." The men she'd come here to study manipulated her constantly, or tried to. Why should she expect Hugo to be any different? Especially with the way their first meeting had gone!

"He's very nice whenever I see him in the dining hall." Lorraine put a sack lunch on the desk. She came up to the administration offices quite often to make sure Evelyn had food to eat, regardless of the meal.

Evelyn peeked in at her lunch: carrots, an apple, a cup of chicken noodle soup and a chocolate-chip cookie. "You can't trust nice." Jasper had once been nice, too. And look what he'd done.

Lorraine adjusted an earring that was hanging too low. "Dr. Fitzpatrick says everyone dons a mask. With psychopaths, that mask is more like a mirror. Whatever they think you want to see, that's what they reflect back at you. They're empty."

No, not empty. Evelyn didn't believe that for a second. She'd once seen the bared soul of a psychopath, stared into his eyes in a way Dr. Fitzpatrick never had and, God willing, never would. The men they treated were far from empty; empty was too synonymous with neutral, harmless. If she were a religious person she might substitute *soulless* and find it quite fitting, but she hadn't been to church in over a decade.

"They know how to blend in," she corrected. "How to appear as emotionally invested as those around them. They're wolves in sheep's clothing, which is why they're able to cause so much pain and destruction." And why the truly caring individuals involved in their lives usually suffered for it.

Lorraine seemed to measure Evelyn more closely. "Are you sure it's only Hugo that's got you down? You look...frazzled."

And it was only Monday. Not a great way to start out the week. "I didn't sleep well last night."

"Why don't you go home and lie down, get some rest?"

Evelyn waved her off. "It's not even noon."

"Listen, this place won't fall apart if you take a couple of hours. Everyone admires your commitment—no one more than me—but you'll run yourself into a brick wall if you don't slow down."

Evelyn shook a daily vitamin from the bottle she kept in her desk and tossed it back with a drink of water. "Don't be so dramatic. I'm fine. And I *can't* leave." She checked the clock hanging on her wall. "Our new inmate will be here any minute."

"Anthony Garza? I thought he wasn't due until four."

"Weather report says we've got another storm coming in. So they caught an earlier flight. You didn't get the message?"

Lorraine adjusted her hair net. "I haven't checked my email this morning. I've been too busy in the kitchen."

"One of the federal marshals called just before I met with Hugo. The plane's already landed in Anchorage." Because of the amount of security required to move the high-profile killers they often received, arrivals were always a big deal. The entire onsite staff was alerted...just in case—although Lorraine's presence wasn't as high a priority as the warden, the correctional officers and the mental health team. The last thing they needed was for someone to make a careless mistake that would result in an escape or injury. As the first institution of its kind, Hanover House was perceived to be a radical new approach to the psychopathy problem, which meant they had to prove themselves professional and effective or risk losing the public support they'd worked so hard to achieve. Just because Hilltop hadn't mounted much resistance to having a maximum-security mental facility built on the outskirts of town—nothing like the other locations the government considered—didn't mean they wouldn't rally at the prodding of an inciting event. For the most part, the locals who weren't working at the center seemed to be reserving judgment, but they weren't welcoming her or her brainchild with open arms, especially Amarok, the handsome Alaska State trooper who was about the town's only police presence.

"What do we know about Garza?" Lorraine asked.

That question made Evelyn uncomfortable. The inmates at Hanover House were hand-selected for the type of crimes they'd committed and the behavior they exhibited. That was one of the details that made their institution unique, besides the friendly name ("house" instead of "prison") and the focus on research and treatment as opposed to simple incarceration. But Evelyn had chosen Garza just because he was so difficult to handle. Had the team been asked to weigh in on some of the details, as they probably should've been, they would've rejected him on the grounds that he was too antagonistic to be considered for their program. Not only had he attacked every cellmate he'd ever had, a year ago he'd nearly killed a guard.

But Evelyn thought that anger, that level of hatred and vocal interaction, might bring insights they'd been missing so far.

"We know he killed the first three of his four wives.

That he's egocentric, feels no real human attachment, has delusions of grandeur and lies like a rug." She straightened her blotter. "He also has a penchant for self-mutilation, but that's another thing."

"How'd he murder his wives?" Lorraine's expression suggested she didn't really care to know but had to ask.

His file lay on the corner of the desk. Evelyn had read the documents inside it several times. She slid it over and flipped through the pages as she spoke. "He didn't do anything uniquely gruesome. Knocked them out with a hammer before setting the bed on fire."

"He did that to all three?"

When she came to a picture of the burned remnants of a mobile home, Evelyn paused. She hated to imagine what'd happened to the poor woman who'd been inside but couldn't stop the heartbreaking images that flashed before her mind's eye. "Yes."

"He wasn't afraid *three* fires would raise his chances of being caught?"

Evelyn managed a shrug as she closed the file. She had to keep some distance between her emotions and what she encountered every day or she would never survive this job. Even if she couldn't maintain that separation, she faked it. Otherwise her colleagues would be all over her—cautioning her, giving advice, telling her she was taking her job too seriously. What she didn't understand was how they could take the men and issues they dealt with any less seriously, how they could look at their jobs as just a nine-to-five grind. "He killed each one in a different state, and he nearly got away with it. Was only tried two years ago, five years after the death of the last woman. By then, he was separated from his fourth wife. I guess he found something that worked and stuck with it."

Lorraine made a clicking sound with her tongue. "Amazing that these cases aren't connected sooner. What about the last wife? Why didn't he kill her?"

"Courtney Lofland? I have no idea." Evelyn set the file aside. "She's remarried and living in Kansas."

"Lucky girl. I bet you'd love to talk to her, see what she has to say about Garza's behavior."

"I've already sent a letter," Evelyn said with a smile.

Lorraine shook her head. "I should've known. With you, no stone goes unturned."

Evelyn ignored the reference to her diligence because she knew the compulsion she felt had turned to obsession long ago. "If she agrees to be interviewed, I'll fly out there and meet her."

"And get away from all this?" Lorraine spread her arms to indicate the sprawling, two-story complex, of which Evelyn's office comprised only a small part of the third wing.

Outside, snow was falling so heavily Evelyn could no longer make out the Chugach Mountains. They'd had sixty inches since she arrived in September, and it was only January thirteenth. "It'd be nice to feel the sun, warm up," she admitted.

"I wish I could go with you. I haven't been much farther from home than the prison."

Evelyn pulled her gaze from the window. "You'd have to fight off the mental health team first. They'd all love to return to the lower forty-eight." Homesickness was what had driven Ely Brand back to Portland, where he was from. That and it wasn't easy adjusting to such a hostile environment. The echoing halls, clanging doors, occasional moans or crazy-sounding laughter were hard enough to cope with. Add to those realities the long dark winter and lonely evenings spent with more files and psychology journals than people, and the memories of countless conversations filled with blood-curdling details, and saying life here was harsh went well beyond the weather.

"Will you take one of them along?" Lorraine asked.

Evelyn shook her head. "We don't have the funds. I'll be lucky if the Bureau of Prisons approves *my* ticket."

"So who'll be working with Mr. Garza?"

"Who do you think?"

"Not you—you're already juggling a lot more than the others. As it is you don't get time to think about anything besides your patients."

Evelyn offered her a rueful smile. "Maybe you haven't noticed, but there's not a lot to do in Hilltop besides work, especially this time of year."

"You could get a social life."

"Which would include...what? Drinking at The

Moosehead?"

"Why not?"

Evelyn had gone there once last summer, before Hanover House even opened. Amarok had taken her. She'd had a good time, but she tried not to think about that.

"You never know what kind of guy you might meet," Lorraine added by way of enticement.

She rolled her eyes. "Truer words were never spoken."

"I meant that you might run into someone fun and interesting, not dangerous."

Like Amarok. Surely Lorraine had heard the rumors about them. Or maybe not. As with so many other members of the staff, she lived in Anchorage and commuted. Didn't socialize with the locals. "There are no guarantees."

"Glenn would go with you."

Glenn Whitcomb, one of the correctional officers, had taken it upon himself to look after the both of them, as well as some of the other women who worked at Hanover House. When he could, he walked them out of the prison, carried anything that was heavy or helped scrape the snow off their cars. "Glenn faces the same drive you do," she said. "He doesn't need to be staying here in Hilltop any later than his work requires."

"Why not? What's he got to go home to? His married sister? He needs to find a mate, too."

"He'll meet someone eventually." Regardless, she

couldn't become any friendlier with him. She could sense how much he admired her, had to be careful. He was lonely, but getting too chummy with a guard wasn't professional and could undermine her authority at HH.

"Come on," Lorraine said. "You have to overcome the past at some point."

She was spitting Evelyn's own words back at her. "I've made peace with my past. I'm happy as I am," she responded, but she knew she bore more scars than the one on her neck. After the attack, she'd spent nearly a decade in therapy.

"You'd rather be single for the rest of your life?" Lorraine asked.

Suddenly realizing that she was hungry, Evelyn pulled the carrots out of the sack. Maybe if she ate something she'd get her second wind. "I don't need a man. I've filled my life with other things."

"Psychopaths?"

"A *purpose*," she said, tearing open the plastic. "And to fulfill that purpose, I can fit one more inmate into my schedule."

Lorraine *tsked*. "You're pushing too hard. Driving yourself right over the edge."

"I appreciate the warning—and the lunch," she said. "What would I do without you in all of this? But I'm okay. Really. So...did Glenn's uncle get your security alarm installed?"

Lorraine gave her a look that let her know she recognized the deliberate change in subject. She allowed it, however. "Last week. That high-pitched tone that goes off when I open the door about makes me jump out of my skin."

Evelyn chuckled. "You get used to it." She could speak with confidence, because Glenn's uncle had also installed one in her house. She found the sound quite comforting.

"I guess it's a wise thing to have."

"It is." Especially because Lorraine's husband had moved out six months ago, and she was now living alone. Evelyn thought it might provide her with some peace of mind—once she became accustomed to how it worked.

"I'd better get back downstairs before all hell breaks loose," Lorraine said. "But I wanted to ask you...have you heard anything from Danielle?"

"Connelly? The gal you hired to help in the kitchen? Not yet. Why?"

"She didn't come in this morning."

"Have you tried calling her house?"

"Of course. Over and over. There's no answer."

"Are you sure she didn't talk to the warden or another member of the team? Maybe she's sick. Maybe she turned off the ringer on her phone so she could get some sleep."

A knock interrupted, right before her assistant, 4'9" Penny Singh, poked her head into the room. "Receiving just called. Anthony Garza has arrived."

"Thank you."

"Did you plan to talk to the marshals?" Penny

asked.

"Of course." Evelyn felt it was important to thank the escorts. Sometimes they had warnings or other information to convey. She also made it a habit to meet with every single inmate as soon as he received his jumpsuit and other essentials so she could create his chart, make some initial notes on his attitude and psychological state and whether he was likely to be a problem.

"You'll have to hurry," Penny prodded. "They can't wait. They're worried about missing their flight, are afraid they'll get snowed in."

Evelyn couldn't blame them for being antsy. With the monstrous cold fronts that rolled through Anchorage, getting snowed in was a real possibility—and it could mean they'd be trapped for a week or longer. "I'm coming." She turned to Lorraine. "About Danielle—can you get away long enough to drive by her house?"

"Not during work hours. Not when I'm short-staffed. But I'll stop on my way home."

"Perfect. Call me if for some reason she's not there."

Lorraine nodded as Evelyn brushed past. But it wasn't fifteen minutes later that Evelyn forgot Danielle. While the staff in receiving checked Garza in, she met with the marshals in the warden's conference room. What they had to say about Anthony made her nervous. So she was already on edge when, right after they left, the intermittent honk of the emergency alarm sounded, punching her heart into her throat.

HER DARKEST NIGHTMARE will be released September 2016, but you don't have to wait until then to enjoy another Brenda Novak novel. THE SECRET SISTER is already out:

Did she once have a sister? Has her mother lied all these years? Why?

After a painful divorce, Maisey Lazarow returns to Fairham, the small island off the North Carolina coast where she grew up. She goes there to heal—and to help her brother, Keith, a deeply troubled man who's asked her to come home. But she refuses to stay in the family house. The last person she wants to see is the wealthy, controlling mother she escaped years ago.

Instead, she finds herself living next door to someone else she'd prefer to avoid—Rafe Romero, the wild, reckless boy to whom she lost her virginity at sixteen. He's back on the island, and to her surprise, he's raising a young daughter alone. Maisey's still attracted to him, but her heart's too broken to risk...

Then something even more disturbing happens. She discovers a box of photographs that evoke distant memories of a little girl, a child Keith remembers, too. Maisey believes the girl must've been their sister, but their mother claims there was no sister.

Maisey's convinced that child existed. So where is she now?

Turn the page to read the first chapter of this engrossing story!

The Secret Sister:
Chapter 1

MAISEY LAZAROW'S BROTHER met her at the ferry—alone. Part of her, a big part, was grateful her mother wasn't with him. Even after ten years, Maisey wasn't ready to confront the autocratic and all-powerful "queen" of Fairham, South Carolina. The fact that Josephine hadn't deigned to come with Keith made it clear Maisey would not be easily forgiven. Only after her mother had punished her sufficiently would she be welcomed back into Josephine's good graces.

Although Maisey had expected as much, coming up against that reality nearly made her balk. What was she doing here? She'd sworn she'd never return to the small island where she'd been raised, that she'd never again subject herself to Josephine's manipulation and control.

But that was before, when she'd set off to build her shiny new life. And this was now, when that shiny new life had imploded on her. She was coming back to Fairham because her brother needed her but, truth be told, she needed Keith, too.

At least her mother wasn't currently married. The men Josephine chose were almost as bad as she was, just in different ways.

What Maisey needed most was her father, she realized as she stood at the railing, peering through the passengers crowding the gangway.

Breathing in the island air, smelling the salty ocean and wet wood of the wharf, it all reminded her of him. But Malcolm had died in a boating accident when she was ten. That was when her mother had grown even more overbearing. Without Malcolm, there was no one to soften Josephine's sharper edges, no one to hold her in check. Not that the buffer he'd provided was the only reason, or even the primary reason, she missed him...

"There you are!" Keith called across the distance, waving to make sure he had her attention.

Grabbing the handles of her two suitcases, which contained everything she hadn't shipped to the island in boxes, she stepped into the flow of people so she could disembark. It was too late to change her mind about moving home. She'd given up her apartment in Manhattan and depleted most of her savings, thanks to the exorbitant fees of the divorce attorney she'd had to hire.

"You look great," Keith told her as she moved closer.

Maisey conjured up her best approximation of a smile—she seemed unable to smile spontaneously these days—and embraced him. "Thanks." She was wearing an expensive white tunic with Jimmy Choo shoes and Chanel jewelry, but she'd never looked worse and she knew it. She hadn't been sleeping or eating well—not since that day two years ago, the worst day of her life. It didn't help that her brother was also going through a difficult time. Once she'd learned about his suicide attempt, she'd been so manic about selling her furniture and what she could sacrifice of her other belongings so she could return to Fairham to be with him that she hadn't bothered to do much shopping or cooking, which had caused her to lose even more weight. Her color wasn't good, either.

But her brother didn't look much better. Nearly six-foot-six with a set of broad shoulders that gave him a nice frame, he could stand to gain some weight, too. And he had dark circles under his eyes—the same blue-green eyes she possessed that always drew so much attention.

"You look good, too," she lied, and suppressed a wry chuckle. She was home, all right. The pretense was already starting. Her ex-husband's frank honesty was one of the things that had attracted her to him, which made his actions at the end of their marriage seem especially ironic.

"How was your trip?" Keith pulled her thoughts away from the past, where they resided far too frequently.

"Not bad," she replied. No way did she want to regale him with stories of how difficult she found it just to walk out of her apartment building. She'd spent weeks at a time holed up in bed, but he didn't need to know that only the urgency of his situation had been sufficient motivation to get her on her feet again. "How's Mom?"

He shot her a look that acknowledged the tension any reference to Josephine created. "The same. She might not act like it, but she's excited to have you home. She's had a room in the east wing prepared for you."

The guest wing? The significance of that didn't escape Maisey. If there'd been any doubt that she was to be treated with cool disdain until she'd done her penance, this proved it.

The anger that flared up, making her stiffen, surprised Maisey. Apparently she wasn't completely cowed and broken. The idea of walking into Coldiron House—named after Josephine's father, Henry Coldiron, who'd owned most of the island before Josephine inherited it—brought back a hint of her old defiance. She couldn't cope with living there, couldn't submit, as she would have to submit, in order to regain her mother's approval.

"I won't be staying at Mom's," she said.

Keith had started to reach for her suitcases. At this, he straightened. "What do you mean?"

"I mean I have to find somewhere else."

He measured her with his eyes, and she found them so hollow she grew frightened for him all over again. Was he doing as well as he claimed? He didn't seem to be particularly robust—in body or spirit.

"I understand it'll be a bit uncomfortable for you at

first." He glanced away as if he could tell she was trying to see behind the front he was putting on. "But trust me. Mom will come around. You'll piss her off if you don't stay at the house, and that'll only make matters worse. After a few weeks..."

"No." She broke in before he could get any further into his appeal. "I can't do it."

He stared at her. "You're serious. You've barely arrived, and you're going to make her angry? She has too much pride to put up with the rejection."

"She rejected me first. And I don't have a relationship with her, anyway,"

Maisey said. "We communicate through email or her housekeeper, for crying out loud. I've spoken to her only a handful of times over the past decade." And when they had talked, there'd been more silence than anything. There'd even been silence when Maisey had desperately craved consolation.

"You need her," he said. "We both do. And that means we'll always be under her thumb."

Although she was secretly frightened that might be true, Maisey scoffed at it. "No. I'll help you, stand by you. I just need to...to get back on my feet, and she can only hurt my ability to do that." The thought of walking through those heavy doors, dragging her belongings behind her, almost gave her a panic attack. At least, if she didn't stay at Coldiron House, she'd retain some autonomy, some independence.

She had to protect the little peace of mind she had

left. He rubbed his gaunt face. "So where will you stay?"

"I could rent a room from someone in town." She had enough money for that, didn't she? Her reserves would last six months or so...

"Here on Fairham?" Her brother shook his head, adamant. "That would provoke an all-out war."

He was right. To maintain some semblance of peace, she couldn't cross certain lines. She couldn't embarrass her mother by revealing that there was any strain inside the family. Appearances were everything to Josephine. They were Coldirons, even though their surname was technically Lazarow, and they needed to comport themselves as such.

How many times had she heard that lecture?

"What if I got an apartment in Charleston?" she asked, but decided against it almost as soon as the words passed her lips. Charleston would cost too much and, left on her own, she wouldn't recover. Being sequestered in a cheap, unfamiliar apartment would be worse than living alone in New York with the furniture Jack hadn't taken.

"I don't see..." he started, but she cut him off again.

"Wait." The solution had occurred to her, and it was so obvious she couldn't believe she hadn't thought of it before. "Why couldn't I stay in one of the bungalows?"

"The vacation rentals? They're on the far side of the island!"

"So?" Going back and forth to Coldiron House

wouldn't require a ferry, like it would from Charleston. And it was September, when the small influx of vacationers who visited Fairham each summer returned to their regular lives. One of the nine units should be available. "We're talking ten miles if I take the bike path. I'll buy a bike and ride over whenever you want me to. Or you can come hang out at my place."

Maisey felt that would be even better. Not only would living in Smuggler's Cove enable her to avoid their mother, it would provide Keith a place to go occasionally, a place where he wouldn't have to deal with Josephine—meaning he wouldn't have to resort to drugs as his escape.

"Most of them haven't been refurbished since Hurricane Lorna last fall," he said.

"I could've sworn you told me months ago that Mom was hiring a contractor." That was well before Keith's last big blowup with Josephine, when he'd stormed off to "live his own life." He'd disappeared for several months before ending up on another drug binge, which had culminated in the black moment that had brought him home again—the same black moment that had ultimately brought her home, too.

"She has hired a contractor," he said, "but she didn't get around to it until I got back a couple of weeks ago. Construction's just begun."

Her mother had waited a year to rebuild? "Why'd she wait so long?"

He took her suitcase, and walked toward the sleek

gray Mercedes he'd parked in the lot. It was their mother's car. He no longer owned anything to speak of.

Although he'd turned thirty-six in February, an age by which most people had managed to accumulate a vehicle and some furniture or other personal property, he'd sold everything for drug money. What he hadn't sold, he'd given away while he was high or destroyed out of anger and frustration.

"She was in another relationship with some off-islander, so she couldn't be bothered," he said in response to her question. "But I'm sure she'll tell you the delay was all my fault. As you know, I haven't made things easy on her—or anyone else."

Including himself... Keith had caused nothing but heartache. But it disturbed Maisey that her mother always had to assign blame. "The future doesn't have to be a reflection of the past." She touched his arm for encouragement. "We'll get through the coming months together. It'll be okay now that we have each other."

When he didn't respond, Maisey wished she hadn't questioned him about the delay in construction, hadn't made him accept responsibility for it. He needed to look ahead—not behind. "I'm sure the bungalows will be ready by next summer, which means we only missed one tourist season."

He was putting her suitcases in the trunk, so she couldn't read his expression. "That's the goal," he said.

"Have you been out to see them recently?" she asked as they slid into the sun-warmed interior of the

Mercedes and buckled their seat belts.

"Mom's sent me over once or twice, yeah." "How bad are they?"

"Pretty bad."

She cringed. "Structurally?"

"Units 1 to 4 need structural repairs."

"What about 5 to 9?" They were set back off the beach, in the trees. Maisey assumed the wind hadn't hit them as hard.

"They're sound, but they still need a lot of work."

Maisey hated that the bungalows had been damaged. Since the eighties, when her father'd had them built, Smuggler's Cove had been a magical place for her, a place where she could find him, or some essence of him, even after he was gone. She had so many fond memories of tagging along to the rentals that, when he died, she'd wanted to scatter his ashes there on the beach. But her mother retained control of his remains, like she did everything else. His ashes were kept in a decorative urn on the mantel of the formal living room at Coldiron House. Not for any sentimental reason. But because it allowed Josephine to pretend he was her one great love, since she hadn't been able to get along with anyone else—not for long, anyway. Every other relationship had fallen apart within two or three years.

"I don't mind helping with the cleanup and repairs, maybe doing some painting, that sort of thing." There was a period when she and Jack, her ex-husband, had watched almost every do-it-yourself show on TV, and used much of what they'd learned to improve their small cabin in the Catskill Mountains. It had been sold, as stipulated by the divorce decree, but she'd always loved it there.

Keith backed out of the parking space. "I'm not sure the contractor's going to like having you in the middle of everything."

"I'll stay out of his way." She tucked her dark hair behind her ears. It was getting too long; she needed to have it trimmed. "Who'd Mom hire? Anyone from around here?"

"Raphael Something. Can't remember his last name. I didn't ask where he was from. I know he's done other work on the island, though, because I've seen his sign—High Tide Construction."

Maisey had never met anyone by that name or heard of the company. But then, plenty could've changed since she'd been gone. "Can we go to Smuggler's Cove now, see if it's even a possibility?"

He hit the brake, stopping before they could exit the lot. "You're not thinking of moving in without asking Mom..."

Knowing that she had a viable alternative—if she did have one—would help her get through that daunting first encounter. "I can't imagine she'd refuse to let me live in one of Dad's bungalows. He'd turn over in his grave if she did." They were something her father had created and paid for with the money he'd brought remember?"

"If she follows his wishes."

Maisey had to acknowledge that the future of the cottages rested in her mother's hands, since Josephine had inherited them first. "Well, you've heard the cliché—it's easier to ask forgiveness than permission."

He pursed his lips. "Not with her."

The complexity of Keith's relationship with Josephine accounted for a lot of his problems. Maisey wished he could get out on his own so he wouldn't need Josephine's help. Then he could also reject her advice and any unwanted intrusions into his life. But, so far, that hadn't happened; he and Josephine were mutually dependent on each other. She provided financial support, and since she couldn't be satisfied with any of her romances, he gave her companionship—when he wasn't acting out. They loved each other but hated each other, too. But because Maisey was coming home with almost nothing, she wasn't exactly the perfect example of how to get away, so she hesitated to say too much.

"Come on, I'm on her shit list, anyway," she said, pretending more indifference than she felt.

He released a sigh. "Fine. Then why not really piss her off, huh?"

Purchase your copy of The Secret Sister today!

About Brenda Novak

New York Times & *USA Today* Bestselling Author Brenda Novak is the author of more than fifty books in a variety of genres, including contemporary romance, romantic suspense and historical romance. A four-time Rita nominee, she has won many awards, including the National Reader's Choice, the Bookseller's Best, the Book Buyer's Best, the Daphne, and the Holt Medallion. When she's not writing, she's usually raising money for diabetes research (her youngest son has this disease). To date, she's raised $2.4 million and would love nothing more than to see a cure in her lifetime. For more about Brenda, please visit www.brendanovak.com.

To subscribe to Brenda's email list, go to
www.brendanovak.com

Find Brenda on the web at www.brendanovak.com
Facebook: @AuthorBrendaNovak
Twitter: @Brenda_Novak
Email: brenda@brendanovak.com